BONE TALK

CANDY GOURLAY

David Fickling Books

31 Beaumont Street
Oxford OX1 2NP, UK

Bone Talk

is a
DAVID FICKLING BOOK

First published in Great Britain by
David Fickling Books,
31 Beaumont Street,
Oxford, OX1 2NP

Hardback edition published 2018
This paperback edition published 2019

Text © Candy Gourlay, 2018
Cover illustration © Kerby Rosanes, 2018

978-1-78845-018-8

1 3 5 7 9 10 8 6 4 2

Papers used by David Fickling Books are from well-managed
forests and other responsible sources.

DAVID FICKLING BOOKS Reg. No. 8340307

A CIP catalogue record for this book is available from the British Library.

Typeset in 11½/16½pt Baskerville by
Falcon Oast Graphic Art Ltd, www.falcon.uk.com
Printed and bound in Great Britain by Clays, Ltd., Elcograf S.p.A.

In loving memory of Dad
Orlando L. Quimpo

And also (with no disrespect to Dad)
remembering my beloved Chuka.
Good dog.

Bontok, 1899

Part One
How to Be a Boy

1

Little Luki and I were tossing pebbles into the eye socket of a water buffalo skull when Father came to fetch me.

He didn't scold or shoo us away. He just looked at me with an odd crumple in his mouth that was almost a smile.

'Samkad, the ancients want you,' he murmured.

Then he swung around and began marching back to the House for Men, so briskly that the axe at his waist slapped a little rhythm on his bare thigh.

'Do I have to?' I complained – although, of course, I didn't say it loud enough for Father to hear.

Little Luki spun gracefully on one toe and flicked another pebble at the skull fixed up high on the blackened tree fern that marked the entrance to our village. Her pebble rattled noisily inside the skull before dropping out of its long bony snout.

'Yah!' Little Luki cried. 'I win!'

'No you don't!' I snapped.

'You can't win if you're leaving!' she retorted. Under its great curling horns, the skull stared at me with sad, empty eyes.

'Samkad!' Father called from several houses up the path.

'Heh!' Luki tossed another pebble, expertly kneeling on one scabby knee at just the right moment to catch it as it shot out of the snout. 'Old Dugas probably needs someone to scratch the soles of his feet so he can sleep. Or maybe Salluyud needs you to pick up the dog droppings in the courtyard!'

I lunged and Luki dodged, but not before I managed to grab her arm and wrestle her down into the dirt, giggling hysterically.

But then she pushed me away, her face suddenly serious. 'Wait, Samkad! What if it's about the snake?'

I sat back on my heels. I had not thought of that.

The day before, Luki and I had found a dead snake between the toes of an old banyan tree. Who could resist? We tied the snake to the end of a string and lay it across the path to the rice valley, carefully covering it with leaves before hiding out of sight behind a large boulder.

Soon enough, along came one of the ancients: Old Pito, whose hair remained long and black despite his wizened little face.

Luki let out a loud *hissssssss* and I tugged the string so that the snake gave a realistic wiggle as it slid across Old Pito's toes.

Pito's long hair puffed up into a wild tangle as he screamed.

His lined forehead screwed into such a twist I thought it would splinter into many pieces. Everyone knows a snake crossing one's path is a warning from Lumawig that evil is about to happen.

'Ah! Ah! Ah!' he cried, whirling about and tottering back to the House for Men. We followed him into the courtyard, struggling to keep our faces serious and straight as we watched Pito and the other ancients pray loudly to our ancestors for help.

I stared at Luki. 'Do you think they found out?' I whispered, thinking of all the horrible punishments the ancients could order upon my head.

'Sam!' Father roared from up the path. 'The old ones are waiting!'

Chickens and dogs scattered as Father strode across the courtyard to the meeting circle where the ancients sat on their heels, each leaning his back against his own stone slab. All four old men were there: Salluyud, Dugas, Pito, Blind Maklan – who stared at me intently with his sightless white eyes bulging between his lids like boiled eggs.

In the rafters above their heads, the skulls of our enemies sneered as if they knew I was in trouble. My belly was aching so hard now that I was bent in the middle. I could already feel a stinging in one palm, as if someone had given it a good hard smack.

'You called me, old ones?' I croaked, forcing my lips to show my teeth.

'Young Samkad,' began Salluyud in a high querulous voice,

as if he was about to begin a long chant. 'How many harvests has it been since you were born?'

'Uh . . .' I looked at Father.

'It has been ten harvests since he was born, old one,' Father said. I peered at him more closely. He looked peculiar; his lips were wobbling like worms.

'Are you all right, Father?'

'Of course I'm all right,' he replied. Wobble.

'Samkad,' Salluyud said. 'It is time.'

Time? Time to punish me for being naughty? I stared hard at my feet as if a grain of rice had suddenly sprouted between my toes.

'Son,' I heard Father say. 'I congratulate you.'

My head snapped up.

All the ancients were grinning so widely, I could see the gums at the backs of their jaws.

'Young Samkad,' Salluyud declared. 'The time has come for you to become a man!'

From somewhere behind me, I heard Little Luki gasp aloud.

I opened my mouth to reply, but no sound came out. I shook my head, which suddenly felt like it was full of air.

'Samkad.' It was Dugas speaking now. 'Are you ready to become a man?'

Pito glared at me solemnly. 'And are you ready for the Cut?'

The Cut. I swallowed.

'Don't be afraid.' I felt Father's elbow nudge me gently on the shoulder.

8

'Why should I be afraid?' I tried to sound scornful, but then my belly groaned so loudly it startled a small bird nearby into flight.

'The Cut will hurt,' Father said. 'But only for a day or two. Don't worry, Salluyud will give you chew leaves to relieve the pain.'

When, years ago, my friend Tambul was given the Cut, we could all hear him howling so that Father had to go behind the House for Men and hold him down. When Tambul waddled out at last with his legs wide apart, I had called: 'What's it like, Tambul? What's it like to get the Cut?'

Tambul didn't answer, making his way to the House for Men where he hid for the rest of the day, as well as the day after that. And the day after that.

Now you are ready to become a man, Sam, I told myself. *And if you're ready to become a man, you are ready to have the Cut.*

'I am ready,' I said aloud, squaring my shoulders and puffing out my chest. 'Lumawig be praised.'

'Lumawig be praised,' Salluyud replied. 'That is good! Tomorrow morning, you and your father will offer a chicken at the Tree of Bones. When you return, I shall take my bamboo knife and—' He clenched his bony fist and gave it a quick flick as if he had the knife in his hand.

I flinched. But I was dying to turn around and look at the expression on Luki's face. How many times had Luki said the ancients would not be calling me to become a man soon? She was so wrong! But I had to force myself to stand still and

9

thank the ancients leaning towards me, their old bones snapping like dried twigs, and say, yes, I am ready for the honour and thank you, thank you, thank you a thousand times.

When the ancients turned away at last to mutter about some other thing, I spun round. Luki was scowling so hard her face looked like a wrinkled old mango.

She began to scold. 'What were the ancients thinking? You're too young! You're too short to carry a shield. You're smaller even than a wild boar – how are you supposed to spear one? And look at your arms! They're like twigs. How are you going to chop off the heads of our blood enemy, the Mangili?'

'Don't be an idiot. I will grow. I am growing right now,' I said. 'And once I'm a man, I will grow faster and become stronger. I'm already stronger than you.'

'No you're not.'

'Yes I am.'

'And you will be allowed to marry. What woman will have you?'

'I will become more handsome, like Tambul,' I said.

Luki's sceptical eyes roamed my face as if she was making a survey of all my unattractive qualities. My cheeks warmed.

'Even if I don't become handsome, someone will want me eventually,' I continued. 'Look at all the husbands in the village. Bagta has smelly armpits. Pulo is half the size of his wife. Ginubo is triple the width of his! And none of them are much to look at.'

'Hah!' Luki's nose curled into a little knot. 'Bet you're going to squeal like a baby when you get the Cut.'

'You're just jealous.' Fury was swelling up inside me now, filling my belly and puffing out of my nostrils. 'Because you're never going to be a warrior. You will always be a girl!'

Luki's mango face twisted hard and her fist connected painfully with my shoulder.

As we wrestled in the dirt, I thought regretfully that this was the very last time I could allow myself to enjoy a good brawl with Luki. Tomorrow I was going to become a man . . . and no self-respecting man in Bontok would fight a girl – even a girl like Little Luki.

2

The next morning I snapped awake before the roosters had even begun to crow. I stared up into the thatch, feeling the tiny imprints of Luki's knuckles on my body from yesterday.

Father was standing over me, as if he'd been waiting by the side of my bed all night. In his hands was a bunch of enormous boar tusks.

I opened my throat to speak, my voice coming out in a croak. 'Are those for—'

'They're for you,' he said, holding up an arm band made of the long, hooked tusks of wild boar. It shone in the quivering light of the fire in the room next door. Father smiled at me so fondly I almost looked away. 'Heh, you're so skinny you might as well wear it around your waist.'

He was right. The band was made for an arm far more muscly than mine. I helped Father put it on. It promptly slipped down to my elbow and, to my shame, Father had to secure it to my stick arm with a piece of string.

When I was small, I had thought that on the day of the Cut, I would suddenly grow tall like a giant bamboo, my voice would deepen and my jaw would prickle with stubble, hair sprouting out of nostrils and armpits – just like my friend Tambul, who had changed quickly after he got the Cut. One moment he was bony and small. The next, he was tall as a banana tree with feet, big as crocodiles.

Father made me take off the rough dirt-coloured breech-cloth made of tree bark I had worn since I was little and handed me a red one made out of cotton. I buried my face in it.

'You're supposed to wear it between your legs, boy!' Father laughed. 'I swapped it with a trader I met in the next village. He'd just returned from the lowlands with a basket full of cotton.'

'What did you swap for it?' I asked as Father helped me put it on.

'Salt,' Father said, tossing my old one into the kitchen fire.

Salt! The thought of Father squandering precious salt on me filled me with guilt.

'Come on, Sam,' Father said. 'Let us get to the Tree of Bones before the sun wakes up.'

The boar-tooth armband jangled noisily on my arm as I followed Father out of the hut's low wooden door. Father didn't linger, marching quickly down the narrow stone lane that meandered between our neighbours' houses. He grabbed one of the chickens by the House for Men and tucked it under his armpit. It glared at me angrily.

Don't look at me like that, chicken, I thought. *Soon you'll be enjoying a new life in the world of the spirits.*

The morning mist was thick around the sleeping village, the tall conical thatched roofs of our huts poking out of the swirling white like so many floating mountains. Our little village was draped like a cat over the mountain's knee. To the east lay deep, sloping valleys that our long-ago ancestors chopped into giant steps for growing rice. To the west, the trail plunged deep into a mossy forest, in the heart of which stood the Tree of Bones.

Father turned to look at me. There was enough light now in the dim, misty swirl to see him clearly. I could see the bright red beak of the hornbill skull fixed above his brow, the tall rooster feathers arching at the back of his head, the axe hanging from his waist. The tattoos all over his torso gleamed in the muted light. Lizards writhed on both shoulders. A caterpillar undulated across his breast. Snake scales were etched on his belly. Around his neck, he wore a necklace made of crocodile teeth.

He looked dangerous and amazing.

We walked down, down, down to the mossy forest. As we marched into its deep shadow, the scents of the wood – of pine, of night beasts, of blossoming flowers – seemed to sharpen even as visibility waned. I could see nothing now. Where were all the trees? Where were the boulders that flanked the trail? I spread my toes like a monkey and flattened the souls of my feet, feeling my way via the prickle of stone and the soft squelch of mud.

Father spoke suddenly, making me jump. 'Don't worry – the sun will awaken soon.' It sounded like he was talking right into my ear, even though he was several lengths ahead of me.

The kindness in Father's voice filled me with guilt. Yesterday, I had come to the ancients fearing that they would punish me for my prank on Old Pito. And now here I was, accepting the greatest honour a boy was entitled to receive.

'Father,' I said softly. 'I have to tell you something.'

And I told him how we had laid the dead snake out, how we had made it wriggle in front of Pito, how Luki had made a loud hissing noise and how the ancient had turned right round and hobbled straight back to the House for Men to pray.

When I'd finished, Father was silent.

'Pito believed that it was Lumawig who sent him the snake, but it was only us,' I whispered. 'I am sorry, Father.'

Father's shadow began to shudder. 'Father, are you all right?' I cried out, alarmed.

And then I realized that he was chuckling.

And then he was laughing out loud, so hard he began to gasp, unable to draw a breath between each chortle. The chicken squawked and clucked.

'Did you really do that?' he laughed. 'You and that Little Luki are impossible! Come here, son.'

In the darkness his strong, hard arm wrapped around my shoulder, pulling me close. The chicken's feathers scratched against my chest.

'The snake was dead when you found it. Its spirit was already gone. You did it no harm,' Father whispered softly. 'And the ancients? They would have been praying to the spirits anyway. As for Lumawig . . . Lumawig created the earth. He gives us day and night, heat and cold, rain and drought. Why would such a powerful ancestor become upset over such a little prank?'

I wanted to throw my arms around Father's neck like a baby. Instead I straightened my back and squared my shoulders. Father ruffled my hair.

'Let's keep moving,' he said. 'Heh, look, Lumawig has roused the sun at last. It's beginning to get light.'

'Yes, Father,' I murmured, tripping over a tree root.

Father was right, though. The sun had begun to edge up the mountain behind us, outlining everything in a warm yellow halo. The dark greys of the forest below us turned a vivid green.

My stomach began to ache. It was not the kind of ache you got from belly gas, but from waiting for something momentous to happen. Soon, I too was going to be carrying a spear, an axe and a shield! Soon, I too would have tattoos carved on my body!

We walked into the trees and immediately a deep silence wrapped itself around us. The steady trill of the crickets, the fumblings of creatures in the bushes, the whisper of the breeze, the rustle of leaves – all sound soaked up by the moss that oozed over everything, coating every stone and trickling from the forest canopy in long green beards.

Shining shafts of sunlight were spearing through the leaves

now so that pine needles glowed red in the dirt and towering ferns burned yellow. Moss and vine dripped in hot, glowing tangles. Everything was on fire.

A small black dog uncurled from behind a bush.

'Away!' Father cried, waving the chicken by its feet. 'Away!'

But the dog remained where she was, gazing beyond Father at me, dark eyes shimmering.

'Pah!' Father stepped around her, beckoning me to hurry.

I followed Father and the dog followed me.

'Away!' I called, even though I liked the way her hot panting breath warmed the backs of my legs.

A breeze blew and suddenly there was a faint tinkling.

Father smiled. 'Hear our ancestors calling to you! They are saying: Welcome, Samkad.'

He waved me on and together we walked into a clearing. Waiting in the middle was the Tree of Bones.

It was a crooked monster of a tree, shaggy with moss, its back a mass of knots and scars, with a waist wide enough to hide ten men. Some branches were thick enough to be trees themselves, sinking down to the earth under their own weight, pulling at the tree so that its spine was in a permanent curve and it hunched over the ground as if it was trying to touch its toes. You could climb up on one of those dragging, fat branches and walk from the bottom of the tree to its tangled crown the way you could walk up a mountain.

A fence of bamboo spears circled the trunk, to keep dogs away. Father stepped carefully over it and waved at me to cross.

The dog pressed a cold nose against my knee. I allowed my fingers to brush over her head before I followed Father over the fence.

He cut the chicken's throat. Its soul departed quickly as its blood soaked into the mossy roots of the tree. 'O spirits,' Father prayed. 'Accept this gift: another spirit for your world. We beg your permission to allow this boy to leave childhood behind and become a man.'

Father stepped up onto one of the tree's sunken branches and it bounced under his weight, the tree made a tinkling noise.

'Hear that?' Father whispered. 'They're calling your name: Samkad . . . Samkad.'

I peered up at the snarl of moss above our heads. The tink-ling came from the bones that dangled from every branch of the huge tree, offerings from times past. Small black figures sat on every branch, their white pebble eyes watching. Each carved figure represented the soul of an ancestor. Right at the top of the tree one of the figures leaned out slightly, as if it was trying to get a better look at us. It was smaller than the others, just big enough to fit in my cupped hands. Mother's spirit figure.

We carefully walked up the sagging branch together. And as we made our way up, the tree shook and the bones clattered.

Near the top where the tree became twiggier and more precarious we had to pull ourselves up, hand over hand. Mother's spirit figure watched serenely, its wooden arms folded over its knees.

Father tied the chicken's carcass carefully to Mother's branch. He pulled a strand of polished granite beads from his belt and wound it round the figure's neck. I laid my hands over its head and Father wrapped his great hands over mine.

'Mother, this precious strand belonged to you when you were alive. May you enjoy it in the world of the dead,' he intoned softly. 'Mother, protect our son and grant him the courage and strength he needs to become a man.'

I bowed my head, enjoying the warmth of Father's palms on my hands.

Father paused. I looked up. He was staring at me with a strange expression on his face. The whites of his eyes were suddenly veined with red and his lips hardened into a line.

He snatched his hands away, pulled his axe from his belt and swung it at my head with all his might.

3

Chak! Father's axe struck the bough just behind my skull, the blade embedding itself in the wood.

Something dropped onto my elbow with a hissing noise.

I stared. It was bright green. A snake.

The diamond eyes held mine, mouth opening and closing as if it was trying to tell me something.

And then, suddenly, the eyes emptied of life and the coiling body seemed to dry up, instantly inert as a twig. It slid off my arm into the dapple of shadows below.

Father reached over my head to pull his axe out. Droplets of sweat glistened on his forehead and the lump in his throat bobbed up and down as he scanned the sky.

Now his eyes searched my face. He touched my cheek and his fingers came away red. Snake blood. Father looked at it with glassy eyes. There was a chittering in the foliage above our heads and he startled.

'Omen bird,' Father whispered. 'We must leave. Now.'

So we did.

When it was still dark, we had managed to climb the tree without a single stumble. But now, in the yellow light of day, we faltered and slipped, as if a hundred angry spirits were chasing us.

And maybe they were. Lumawig had surely sent the snake to warn us about something. How Luki and I had laughed at Pito's terror when we played our little trick with the dead snake! But this snake had been alive. It had stared right into my eyes, trying to warn me about something before its soul departed. And then Father murdered it. Surely, Lumawig will punish him for it. I glanced up but the sky was empty. No clouds. No thunderbolts. No scorpions. No stones.

The black dog was waiting for us by the fence. She greeted me with a broad smile, but we ran right past her. She chased after us, barking as if we were running for a game. Father said nothing as we began to climb the mountain to the village. He didn't even glance over his shoulder to make sure that I was keeping up.

We ran past the tree fern with the water buffalo skull. Past the pigs in stone pens, where several men were mixing manure with grass to feed the mud of the rice paddies. Past the House for Women, where girls were pounding rice in a large stone mortar.

The girls shrieked and waved. It was hard to tell if they were greeting or teasing me. I turned my burning face away.

'Sam!' A familiar voice cried. It was Little Luki, who was waiting her turn at the mortar. She quickly rolled her skirt up over her knees and raced after me. 'Is it time? Is Salluyud going to do the Cut?'

She grabbed my arm, but I shook her off.

Her mango face frowned. 'What's wrong? You look like you swallowed a cockroach!'

Before I could say anything, Chochon was there, tugging Luki away. 'No, no, no . . . where do you think you're going, daughter? How many times do I have to tell you to leave the men to their business!'

She dragged Luki back to the mortar. 'Luki wants to be a boy!' one of the girls jeered.

'Better than wanting to be an ugly monkey like you!' I heard Luki yell.

At the House for Men, Tambul was lounging under a tree. When he spotted me, he raised his axe and yelled, 'All praise Samkad, our new man!'

'Come on, Sam!' Father barked over his shoulder.

I hurried past Tambul, looking everywhere except at him. All four ancients were waiting when we arrived at the stone circle. Salluyud stood abruptly and held up his bamboo blade – but the smile slid off his face as Father and I came to a stop, hands on knees, panting.

'What?' the old man cried. 'What has happened?'

Tambul hurried over, trying to catch my eye as Father began to explain.

I couldn't meet his or anyone else's gaze. In my belly, shame and fear were nibbling with tiny pointed teeth.

When Father got to the part where he saw the snake slithering towards me, the ancients all straightened, their spines crunching.

'After it appeared, we heard an omen bird cry out a warning,' Father said. 'We ran back as fast as we could.'

Then he shut his mouth.

Weh! Was he not going to tell them that he chopped Lumawig's messenger in half? That he *killed* it?

Salluyud laid a hand on Father's shoulder. 'Samkad, the snake is our friend,' he said, as if we didn't already know this. 'It would not reveal itself without good reason.'

Maklan blinked his boiled egg eyes. 'You did well to heed these warnings and leave the Tree of Bones.'

Heed the warning? Father didn't heed any warning. He just killed it. I frowned at him, but his eyes avoided mine. *Surely you will tell them what you did, Father. Tell them you killed it. Tell them!*

But Father kept his eyes on the ground.

Now Salluyud was patting my shoulder. 'Young Sam.' He turned me gently towards him. His eyes reflected the fire, tiny, glimmering torches in each pupil. 'Do not fear – the spirits will tell us the right thing to do. We will examine the portents now.'

'Yes. The portents will explain,' Father said quickly then he

23

looked at me. I could see the warning in his eyes: *Don't you dare tell them. Don't you dare.*

Pito fetched a chicken and the four ancients sat close together as Salluyud prepared to send the bird's soul to our ancestors.

Dugas and Pito crowded close as Salluyud cut its throat and exposed its insides with his blade. They muttered to each other as they read the portents left by the bird's spirit.

'What do you see?' Maklan's blind eyes rolled impatiently in his eye sockets.

Tambul once told me that a warrior had to practise hiding his emotions. 'Your face is the great betrayer,' he had explained, 'You must train yourself not to show fear, sorrow, even happiness.'

I glanced at Father. His face was unreadable, like stone.

'We should have known,' Pito sighed, tossing his black mane over one bony shoulder.

Salluyud turned to me. 'Sam, the portents say that like your mother before you, your soul is tied to one other.'

'To one other?' I said. 'To who?'

'Kinyo.' Dugas struck the fire with his cane and I flinched as it sent a shower of tiny sparks over me.

'Kinyo?' I blinked furiously. 'There's nobody by that name in the village.'

'Your soul is tied to his,' Dugas explained. 'You cannot become a man until he returns to Bontok.'

'Kinyo, named after an old warrior.' Salluyud started chanting. The other ancients joined in.

'Kinyo, son of Sipaa, your mother's best friend.'

'Kinyo is tied to your soul the way Sipaa's soul was tied to your mother's.'

Kinyo. Kinyo. Kinyo.

'Father! Make them stop!' I cried. 'I don't know anybody named Kinyo!'

But I was lying.

4

My dead mother's name was Uda and her soul had always been tied to that of her best friend, Sipaa.

Uda and Sipaa. Sipaa and Uda. When I was growing up, everybody in the village was eager to tell me what great friends the two women were.

'Lovely girls, faces smooth as new fruit, hair always festooned with flowers,' remembered old Pito, twirling a lock of his youthful hair. 'Their skirts were exactly the same weave. When one had a flower over her right ear, the other wore a flower over her left.'

'Inseparable!' Dugas said in his complaining voice. 'Like tandem birds always swooping about side by side. It was as if they were tied together by invisible string.'

'How can you turn the soil when you're arm in arm with someone else? How does one thresh rice with another person alongside? But they did it!' Salluyud said, with his barking laugh. 'They did everything together!'

Mother and Sipaa continued to be inseparable when they grew up. They even fell in love at the same time. Mother with Father, and Sipaa with Tomo, who made salt in the hot springs at the top of the mountain.

They continued to do everything together even after they had chosen husbands and moved out of the House for Women into their own homes. They visited the river together to collect water at the same time every day. They did their kitchen jobs together, sitting side by side as they peeled sweet potatoes or prepared the grain.

So when they discovered that they both had babies growing in their bellies, it was said, they became too smug with happiness. 'We truly share one soul!' my mother told everyone.

Uda and Sipaa needed to make an offering to the spirits to make sure their births would go well. But they were so full of contentment and satisfaction that they kept putting it off. They forgot to fear the wrath of the spirit world.

It was not until their bellies were already as round and smooth as river boulders that they remembered they had respects to pay.

They each took a chicken and set off for the Tree. But their bellies were so enormous that the steep downward path to the mossy forest was a struggle. The tree was still a distance away when they struggled to a stop. They could not face the rest of the walk.

Should they return on another day when they were feeling stronger? But even that prospect was exhausting. Surely the spirits would not mind if they left the chickens at the foot of another tree? Surely Lumawig could hear their prayers if they prayed loudly enough?

And that is what they did.

They dispatched their chickens to the spirit world quickly, mumbling their prayers to Lumawig and the ancestors. They left the carcasses there, under that other tree, not far from the Tree of Bones. And went home.

When the ancients scolded them, the two women just laughed. 'Our ancestors will understand,' they smiled, patting their fat bellies. 'All will be well.'

These are our collected memories, the ancients say. This is how we remember: we remember together. And I do treasure those memories of my mother and her friend, of times I did not know. But even more precious are the memories that I do remember, once I was born.

I remember how it hurt to become alive. The inside of my chest stung like a new wound as air filled it for the first time. It hurt on the outside, too – my skin was so new every fresh sensation was like a slap. It hurt when I moved, and it hurt the first time I opened my throat to scream.

I remember when I saw Father for the first time. I can remember the heat of his breath against my face and the way his lips parted to show his teeth. And even though I didn't know what a father or a smile was, it felt good. *He* felt good.

I remember Mother. I had one glimpse of her before Father carried me off to be washed. She lay on a blanket in front of the hearth, smiling. Her eyes were warm. The light from the fire flapped over her like so many yellow butterflies. Beads of sweat glittered on her forehead.

Father tipped ladles of water over me, rubbing me all over with water so cold it made my skin itch. When he was done, Father wrapped me in a blanket and took me back to Mother.

'See, Uda,' he whispered. 'Our son.'

I looked at Mother curiously. Her eyes were closed and her lips were a dark purple in the firelight. This was not the smiling creature I had seen before.

'Uda! Uda!' Suddenly Father was sobbing. He pressed his face against the top of my head. The bones of his face felt hard, and my hair became wet with his tears. I began to whimper. Then he shouted. 'Why are you taking her from me? Why are you calling away her soul?'

Father was frantic. He grabbed a fistful of rice from a basket nearby and scattered it across the floor. I have seen people do this hundreds of times since. A wicked spirit seeking to steal Mother's soul away would not be able to resist counting the grains on the ground.

But then Father fell to his knees, retrieving the grains he'd only just scattered.

'No, no,' he muttered. 'You will not have him as well!'

He had realized that the rice might lead the wicked spirits to me. He didn't want them to steal me too.

Father staggered out of the hut, shouting and calling, begging Lumawig to intercede with the world of the dead. 'Mercy!' he cried. 'Pity this motherless child!' He held me high, and for the first time I gazed up at the night sky, speckled with millions of tiny lights. I saw the moon for the first time, round and yellow.

And then we both became aware of another raw voice. Someone else, weeping and calling. I saw another man in the shadows. He too had a new baby in his arms.

It was not only my mother who had been stolen away that night.

Of course I remembered Kinyo. How could I forget the other boy whose mother was taken on the same night as mine? The spirits took our mothers that first night, and soon after, the news came that Kinyo's father Tomo had been found dead in the forest. Killed by our blood enemy, the Mangili, and his head taken for a trophy.

The ancients rushed to give us names for our own safety, so that our ancestors could protect us from enemy spirits.

My name was easy. 'Samkad', after Father, who took his name from a line of great warrior ancestors.

But the ancients had trouble naming the other baby. It would have been unkind to name the child 'Tomo', after a father whose soul had been dispatched by his enemy.

It took some time but eventually one of the ancients vaguely remembered a distant warrior ancestor named 'Kinyo'.

We had to feed on a thin gruel of rice washing until Father persuaded a woman to allow me to suckle alongside her own babe. 'She only has enough milk for Samkad,' I heard one of the ancients remark. 'There isn't enough for the orphan as well.'

'Perhaps we ought to hand him over to the care of his mother and father in the world of the dead,' another ancient replied.

Gentle fingers brushed against my forehead and I looked up to see Father's eyes gazing wetly down at me. 'No,' he said. 'We must save the boy.'

'But he is not ours to raise!' the ancient cried.

'His aunt will raise him,' Father said.

Kinyo's mother had a sister, younger than her, named Agkus. But Agkus was a troublesome one. She had begged the ancients to allow her to become a trader, even though it was a job for a man, wearing them down with her nagging until they allowed her to carry our goods to other villages. Then she returned from one of her trips and announced that she was going to marry a man from the lowlands.

Of course the ancients opposed the marriage. What? Leave the village? Leave her people? How could she make her home in the lowlands where she had no ancestors to protect her? But Agkus said she was happy to abandon all these things for her man.

'That girl, Agkus?' one of the old men scoffed. 'Pah!'

I had stopped feeding to listen. The milk mother nudged her teat back into my mouth. The baby on her other breast made loud smacking noises. In the background, I could hear Kinyo wailing. It was a thin, exhausted sound.

'He is her blood,' Father said.

'But she has left us. She has chosen to become a stranger.'

'Let me take him to her,' Father said. 'I will journey down to the lowlands and deliver the baby to Agkus. Until then, little Samkad will have to give half his share to his brother.'

Father took me then, away from the nourishing breast. I nuzzled and searched, but there was no more milk for me that day.

Kinyo's cries ceased abruptly as he took my place at the milk woman's breast.

5

I shook my head, pushing the memories aside, and watched the old men poring over the chicken's entrails, shaking their heads. Father hovered behind them, his face grim. People were trickling into the courtyard, curious to know what calamity had happened. I felt like I was shrinking, the stones and trees and houses beginning to loom over my head.

'Fetch another chicken!' Salluyud commanded. Tambul snatched one from the corner of the courtyard and delivered it, squawking, to where the old men sat against their stone rests.

'You mean the portents can change?' I asked.

Dugas nodded, his face kind. 'A snake could be a warning of immediate danger. These new portents will let us know if the danger is over and we can continue with your manhood ceremony.'

Hope surged in my chest. I had been biting my bottom lip so hard I could taste blood.

The ancients called to the spirits in loud voices, praying for favour. Then they quickly sent the bird's soul into the world of the dead and cut the chicken open.

There was a long silence.

'What does it say?' I said in a small voice.

Suddenly all the ancients were looking in different directions.

At last, Salluyud's eyes slid towards me. 'It cannot be done. You cannot have the Cut. This is the message the snake carried for Lumawig,' he said. 'We will have to wait until your soul brother, Kinyo, returns.'

I looked from one face to the other. Wait for a stranger?

'It's a mistake!' I said. 'Are you sure that's what it says?'

Maklan's boiled egg eyes fixed on me. 'Are you doubting the spirits, boy?'

'But . . .' I was panting. 'We've already been to the Tree of Bones. We've already made a promise to Mother!'

'Yes, that is true. That's why we must choose another boy to take your place,' Maklan said, his voice flat.

'Another boy?' I couldn't believe it. Someone else was going to take the manhood that was meant for me. How could that be fair? I turned to Father. Father's hornbill headdress lay abandoned on the ground. I had not even seen him cast it off. He stood, silently, his chin deep in his chest, his eyes closed.

'Father,' I croaked. 'This is your fault.'

His eyes flew open.

'Father!' My voice sliced the air like a spear. 'I would have had a chance if it hadn't been for you! Tell them what you did! Tell them how you angered the spirits and changed the portents!'

The old heads swung towards me, bleary eyes alert.

'What is the boy saying?' Maklan said softly.

'I am saying that you ancients have been DECEIVED!' *But didn't you deceive them too, Samkad?* a voice whispered in my head. *Didn't you play a prank with a dead snake?* I shook my head, pushing my unruly thoughts aside.

Tambul had dropped his pipe and for a moment I thought he was going to grab me and cover my impertinent mouth with his hand. He didn't have to. Father was already striding across the courtyard, his face dark with rage. 'Insolence!' he cried, taking my arm and shaking me like he was shaking fruit from a tree. The boar's teeth armband jangled on my arm and I ripped it off. 'How dare you speak this way? It is unforgivable!'

'Unforgivable?' I was startled by the shrillness of my own voice. 'It was not me who lied to the ancients.'

'Lied?' Salluyud stared at Father.

Father was suddenly still, his eyes darting from side to side.

'You are the liar, Father. Why don't you tell the ancients what you did?' The bitter words were flying out of my mouth with a will of their own. How could I cram them back into my throat once they had escaped?

35

'What are you talking about, boy?' Dugas cried. 'Samkad, what is the boy telling us?'

'I am telling you what Father didn't have the courage to admit! When the snake appeared, he chopped it in half. He killed it. This is why the spirits are denying me my manhood.'

Weh, Father's eyes were so wide there was more white than black. 'Old ones, I can explain—'

The old men just looked at him.

He whirled towards me, his hand thudding onto my shoulder like a club. 'Why are you doing this to me, Samkad?'

'How am I doing this to you?' I cried. 'What about me? Am I to wait until I'm an ancient before I can become a man?'

'I deserve thanks, not blame!' Father spoke from between clenched teeth. 'I killed the snake to give you your life.'

I blinked furiously, trying to stop my tears from spilling over. 'It was not life you gave me, Father, but shame.'

'Sam, all will be well when Kinyo returns!' Father was pleading, his eyes begging my forgiveness. But the sight of his remorse filled me with disgust.

'Kinyo?' I shouted. 'Who is Kinyo? How do you know he will ever come back? How do you even know he's still alive?'

Father's face turned a dull red. 'Don't you dare speak to me like that, Sam. I am your elder. Your mother would be outraged to hear you!'

'My mother!' I laughed wildly. 'What mother? I do not have a mother!'

Father's palm on my cheek made a sharp noise like an earthen pot splintering against a rock.

'I hate you,' I whispered. 'I hate you, Father.'

'Sam . . .' Father held a hand out. Perhaps he wanted to offer me comfort, show that he was sorry, show that he cared.

But I just slapped it away and ran.

6

As I fled with my shame and disappointment, I could hear Father pleading, 'Let me explain! Let me explain!' under the angry clamour of the ancients.

In my desperation, I ran clumsily, catching my elbows on the corners of houses, stubbing my toes on stones and dislodging small boulders that rolled and bounced ahead of me on the downward path as if they were racing me to the mossy forest.

As I dived into the trees, I could hear the distant murmur of the Tree of Bones. Perhaps the spirits were discussing what had happened. Perhaps they were plotting an awful vengeance. Perhaps they were agreeing that I did not deserve to become a man.

'Kind spirits,' I called into the trees. 'It was just a mistake.'

A soft breeze brushed against my cheek and the Tree of Bones chattered louder. 'Mother, help me,' I cried. 'Tell them

Father didn't mean it.' The chatter continued. *If you know Father did not mean it, why did you tell on him?*

'Mother?' I whispered. 'Are you listening?'

The chattering stopped. Had Mother's spirit managed to persuade our other ancestors to spare me?

There was a flicker of movement behind a large tree.

I swallowed. 'Mother?'

A low noise. Something between a throat clearing and a grunt. The sound hardened, as if it came from a throat filled with sharp stones.

A wild boar!

Slowly, slowly, I turned round, trying to spot the beast hiding in the trees. But nothing stirred in the undergrowth, though the grunting continued. I could feel it watching me, waiting for its chance to attack and gouge me with its tusks.

I needed something to defend myself with. I grabbed a branch nearby and tried to snap it off its trunk. But the tree wouldn't let it go.

Tambul once told me all I had to do in case of a boar attack was to punch the boar hard between its tiny eyes and it would turn around and run in the opposite direction.

I stared at my fists. They looked like pebbles on the ends of sticks.

The grunting became even louder. Shriller. I frowned. It sounded like . . . was that giggling?

'Little Luki!' I roared.

There she was, on a branch right above my head, bouncing

up and down with a massive grin on her face. She had taken off her skirt and put on a breechcloth like mine. If her hair had been cut above her brow instead of tucked behind her ears, she would have looked exactly like a boy.

'You know you ought to stop calling me "little",' she laughed. 'I'm the same size as you now!'

I scowled. 'The ancients are going to bury you under an ants' nest when they see what you're wearing!'

'They can't see me now, can they? Nobody can!' Luki blithely slid down the tree. '*You* try wearing a skirt, Samkad, and see if you like it!' She folded her arms across her chest. 'So, tell me, what is going on? Everyone in the village could hear the yelling.'

I told her about Father and the snake in my most matter-of-fact voice, as if I was relaying news about some new method of chasing the rice birds from the fields. I raised my chin and concentrated on keeping my eyebrows straight, bracing myself for the inevitable joke Luki will make out of my misfortune.

But she actually looked dismayed. 'That's terrible, Samkad! You must be so disappointed.'

'I'll survive.' I was annoyed to feel tears starting in my eyes at her sympathy. I looked away, turning my face towards the tree canopy and holding a hand up. 'Did you feel that? A rain-drop!' I made a show of dusting imaginary raindrops off my shoulders.

But Luki was not going to change the subject. She stamped

her foot. 'Your father should have been more careful! And what about those portents? This is not fair.'

It was gratifying to see that she understood my distress. We stood facing each other silently, deep in thought.

Luki's head snapped up.

'Heh, Sam, you don't need a stupid ceremony to become a man. If you want to become a man, then you should just *be* one.'

'Heh,' I scoffed. 'Be a man? What is that supposed to mean? I need the ancients to make it official. Nobody will call me a man without their say so.'

She grabbed me by the shoulders. 'You just need to do something so manly they will have no choice but to treat you like one!'

'Eh?'

'Do what a man does and they will call you a man.'

'And what thing is this that I should do?'

'There are lots of things that make a man. Fight a war. Kill a wild boar. Kill a Mangili!'

How was I supposed to find myself a Mangili? And even if I did, how was I supposed to fight one without a weapon? I shoved Luki hard in the shoulder. 'You don't know what you're talking about!'

Luki shoved me back. 'If you kill a Mangili, there will be no question of your manhood. You know I'm right, don't you, Samkad?'

She was right. The Mangili had been taking our heads and we had been taking theirs since we began to remember. What

41

young man didn't dream of adding a Mangili skull to the rafters of the House for Men?

But I just growled, 'What a stupid idea.'

'Pah!' Luki planted her shoulder in mine and pushed, making those stupid grunting noises again.

'Stop that!' I cried. 'I'm not going to fall for your wild boar prank again!' I stared at her . . . how was she managing to make that noise without moving her lips?

Then I smelled it. A powerful musky reek. The odour of wild boar.

Fearfully, I looked around me.

One of the boulders clustered around a tree was stirring. It heaved itself to its feet, its hackles raised, white tusks gleaming in its hairy black jaws, its tiny red eyes filled with hatred.

Be a man. Kill a wild boar.

I clenched my fists. 'Luki,' I whispered. 'Do you know how to punch a boar?'

But Little Luki was already racing up the hill.

'Run, Samkad!' she yelled over her shoulder.

The boar lowered its head to charge.

I got ready to punch it between the eyes.

But my feet were not having it. They were already pounding after Luki.

When I glanced over my shoulder, the boar had halted its attack and was watching us make our escape. Its lower jaw shook a little, almost as if it was laughing.

*

We ran all the way to the fern tree pillar with the water buffalo skull.

A woman with a full jar of water on her head grabbed Luki's shoulder. 'Girl, why are you dressed like that? Your mother will be furious!'

Luki grimaced, pulling away and hurrying alongside me towards the House for Men. When we were just a few houses away, we stopped to catch our breath.

'You must have known that boar was there!' I gasped.

Before Luki could reply, there was a scream.

'This way!' Luki cried, racing towards the noise.

'Luki!' I called, 'You need to change back into your skirt or the ancients will—' But she had already reached the courtyard.

I followed reluctantly. Father would be furious that I'd run off, the ancients would be pitying and the younger warriors were sure to patronize me while pretending to be sympathetic.

A boy suddenly appeared at the top of the lane. It was Bitteg . . . and the way he waddled, with his legs far apart, made the breath catch in my throat. The ancients had not wasted any time. That squeal had not come from a pig but a boy. While I'd been in the forest with Luki, they had summoned Bitteg and given him the Cut that was meant for me.

But he was younger than me!

But he was smaller!

But it was *my* chicken that had been offered to the ancestors this morning!

But. But. But.

My eyes caught his, but he turned away as he waddled slowly down a lane towards his mother's house.

Shame turned my belly cold. I was totally disgraced now and it was all Father's fault.

'Father!' I roared. 'Father!'

Someone grabbed my arm. 'Calm down, Samkad,' Tambul said kindly. 'Where have you been? Everyone's been looking for you.' The young warrior bent over me, so close I could see the pulse throbbing under the gecko tattoos across his chest.

I shook him off. 'I need to find Father. I must speak to him at once!'

'Samkad,' Tambul said softly. There was pity in his expression. 'That's what I'm trying to tell you. Your father has left.'

'Left?'

'He said it was the only way he could make it up to you,' Tambul said. 'He has gone to the lowlands to fetch Kinyo.'

7

That evening I lay sleepless on the low wooden bed I had shared with Father since I was born. Guilt prickled inside me, like a thorny vine had suddenly sprouted inside my belly, its spiky tendrils coiling and bristling under my skin.

Smoke from the fires of my neighbours crawled in the thatch above my head. It had been warm and dry all day, but now that it was night, the house felt damp and cold.

It was the first time the ancients had not insisted I stay with one of them when Father went away. 'You are old enough to be on your own,' Dugas had informed me.

Old enough to sleep alone, but not old enough to become a man, I thought.

I sighed, pressing a hand to my chest where my heart beat gently. I was sorry now that I had been so petulant. I was sorry that I'd told the ancients that Father killed the snake. I was sorry that I had not spoken to Father before he left for the lowlands.

The way to the lowlands was full of danger. The Mangili prowled outside our borders, hoping to take a Bontok head, all the better to deprive our ancestors of a soul. I pictured Father trudging down, down, down the mountain on his own. There would be no help if the Mangili attacked. And what if a malicious Mangili spirit pushed him over a precipice? Father had put himself in danger for my sake, and if something happened to him it would be all my fault.

I tried not to imagine the cliffs and ravines hiding in the black of night. Tried not to think of the wicked spirits waiting to make mischief on the trail. Tried not to picture the Mangili, lying in wait behind trees and boulders, hoping to chop off Father's head.

'Don't worry – your father is more than a match for our enemy,' Tambul had tried to reassure me. 'And the lowlanders will leave him alone. Everyone knows lowlanders are afraid of mountain people. That's why they never come up here.'

'It is good to fear your enemy,' Father once told me. 'Fear means you take nothing for granted. It is easy to get lulled into a false security, especially if your enemy looks just like you, as the Mangili do.'

'I thought you said they had bright red lips!' I had replied.

Father laughed. 'Yes, they do. And yes, they speak an incomprehensible tongue. And yes, they dig up their dead to clean their bones, and call on their ancestors to shower malice upon us! But we are a match for them. We can defeat them with the help of our ancestors.'

I reached for Father's blanket. Rolled it into a small, vaguely Father-shaped lump and threw an arm over the lump the way I would have thrown an arm over Father's waist.

I dreamed I was lying flat on my back in an open grave. Its walls loomed up around my body and high above me I could see a rectangle of blue sky. There was a heavy rustling and creaking and I watched as the Tree of Bones appeared in the grave's open mouth. It leaned in and a deep gash in the main trunk yawned like jaws. It shook its great shaggy head so that leaves showered into the grave. The bones jangled like sharp, accusing voices.

'Please!' I cried from the grave floor. 'Please!'

The Tree of Bones raised its great head and I saw that the multitude of things dangling from its branches were not bones but snakes. Thousands of them, coiling and hissing, their diamond eyes glaring down at me.

'Snakes, why are you here?' I shouted. 'What are you trying to tell me?' Slowly, they detached themselves from the branches above me. Down they glided, winding round and round the tree's mammoth trunk. And then they were slithering over me, my legs, my arms, my body. Winding themselves tighter and tighter . . .

I stared up into the musty thatch, blackened by smoke, listening to the pounding of my heart. The night air was freezing and yet my forehead was slick with sweat.

So now Lumawig was sending snake messengers in my dreams. He was warning me about something. But what?

I heard a scraping at the door and held my breath. Perhaps the Tree of Bones was waiting there, outside the door, to deliver another snake.

But then I heard a soft whimpering. Slowly, I rose and unlatched the door. A whirlwind of black fur and licking tongue rushed in. It was the dog from this morning. She nudged my hand, whining wretchedly for me to stroke her head. I tried to push her back out of the door, but she darted past me and bounded into the sleeping room and onto the bed, her nose tucked under Father's blanket.

How could I resist? I climbed in and she pressed against the length of me, all warmth and soft fur.

I was glad for her company on the loneliest night of my life. There were plenty of other dogs in the village. Let them be the fierce ones.

8

Nothing more was said about my manhood.

When the ancients selected Luki's mother, Chochon, to cast the rice seeds into the beds at the foot of the mountain, I put a polite smile on my face even though there was no gladness in my stomach.

When the ancients offered another chicken to the spirits and loudly begged them for rain, I shouted along with everybody else and helped the men build a great fire.

When the seed beds thickened with bright green shoots, I joined in everyone's laughing and exclaiming. 'A fat crop!' we cried. 'Our granaries will soon be full!'

I smiled and I celebrated and I prayed. As if I cared that the rice valley was getting enough to drink. As if I cared that the harvest was going to fill our bellies. As if I wanted to please our ancestors. But deep inside I felt nothing but the scratching of that thorny vine.

The moon had been full when Father left. Slowly, it waned to a skinny sliver, as if dark jaws were nibbling away at it in the night. And still Father didn't return.

One day, I made my way up to a stone ridge just above the village, the black dog scrabbling eagerly beside me. Luki appeared out of nowhere and quietly fell in step with us. I did not send her away.

She was dressed in a skirt.

When she'd turned up at the House for Men in a breech-cloth, Salluyud had lectured her. 'Men, women and children should know their place in our community,' he'd said. 'What would happen if everyone decided to do whatever they liked? If one decided they could not be bothered to help with the rice fields. If one decided they did not want to fight the enemy. Our people would be obliterated from these mountains!'

Luki had promised she would dress properly. That she would honour the work of the women. That she would stand with the women up to her knees in muddy water and turn the precious soil.

And so far . . . I glanced at my friend. She seemed to be keeping her word.

We had almost reached the ridge when Luki spoke at last. 'The wind is colder here!'

I shrugged, staring up at the single tree that grew out of a crack in the stone, reaching up and up and up like a giant weed, even though there was only dust and the endlessly blowing wind to nourish it. It whipped about in the fierce gust.

Luki bent to rub between the dog's ears. 'How about we name your dog "Chuka", Sam? It's a nice name, isn't it?'

'Dogs don't have names.'

'But look at her.' Luki took the dog's black face and turned it towards me. 'She wants a name.'

I looked at her. The melting brown eyes gazed lovingly into mine. *Chuka*, I thought. And then shook my head. 'She wouldn't know the name belongs to her.'

'Look at her! She knows it's her name.' Luki whistled. 'Chuka!'

The dog grinned and barked, tail wagging with excitement as if she approved.

I ignored them, marching up to the tree.

'What are you doing?' Luki called.

I grabbed the tree's trunk and pulled myself up.

'I'm not going up there with you,' Luki said.

'I'm not asking you to come,' I replied.

'Why are you climbing, though?'

I didn't answer, pulling myself even higher. I didn't want to explain myself. I didn't want to tell her that I wanted to get as high as I could, that I wanted to see all the way to the lowlands, that I wanted to see whether Father was on his way back on the trail.

'Sam?' A shuddering gust of wind snatched her voice away.

Father once said if you walked right through the forest to the other side and kept on walking until the mountains dwindled,

51

you would come to a broad, raging river. This was where our world ended and the lowlands began – vast, endless flat plains that rolled all the way to the horizon and beyond. I shuddered, finding it hard to imagine. A mountainless place! It sounded strange and desolate.

The river was easy enough to cross, with care and luck, Father had explained. He had done it successfully twice, hadn't he? Over and back, when he delivered Kinyo to his aunt. But it was not a thing to do lightly because the spirits of our ancestors would not follow into the lowlands. There was no one to protect us there. We Bontok relied on the spirits of our ancestors to make sure that our babies were born fat and healthy and not cross-eyed and sick, to keep our houses from being blown away by storms, to guard us against the ancestors of our enemies.

I climbed beyond the safety of the lower, sturdier branches, up, up, up into the sticks and singed leaves at the top.

Far below, I could hear Luki testing the dog's new name. 'Chuka! Chuka!' Her voice was a reedy, distant murmur.

When I could find no more branches that would take my weight, I stopped and surveyed the vista below me.

Our village was a small cluster of thatched rooftops. All around there were water-filled rice paddies, hundreds of them, ranging up and down the mountain, in and out of the mountain's folds, hacked out of the slopes by our ancestors when they were still living men. The irregular shapes were like the patterns on a lizard's back, the glinting blue sky reflected in the diamond scales.

The ancients were selecting the best grain from the granaries to be planted in seedbeds at the mountain's feet. Once the shoots were tall enough, the seedlings would be planted out in the paddies to ripen into grain, turning the lizard scales green. The grain would be harvested, leaving the lizard scales brown with mud. And then the process would begin again.

The path across the terraces was a white, wiggling stripe that followed the contours of the mountain then dropped down into the mossy forest. I could just see it emerging on the other side of the mass of dark green, before it disappeared behind a stony mountain.

I watched the white stripe for any signs of Father while Luki played with Chuka below. Then I climbed down. The next day, I did it again.

The sun rose and fell, rose and fell, rose and fell. The moon slowly fattened up again.

And Father didn't come and didn't come and didn't come.

9

The seedbeds were soon tall with green. It was time to plant the seedlings out into the paddies.

On planting day, leaving Chuka snoring in my bed, I packed a small lunch basket of rice and fish, then hurried to the House for Men. Higher up on the slope, warriors were already in position on dirt mounds, standing guard in case the Mangili decided to attack as we worked in the paddies. Men with great baskets of manure on their head were already making their way carefully across the terraces on the narrow trail.

The sun had only just breached the horizon, but the day had already turned from cold to hot. My neck was prickling with sweat by the time I entered the courtyard where the ancients waited, swaddled in their blankets as if it was the middle of the night.

They seemed half asleep – Salluyud, as usual, toying with

his bamboo knife, Pito, eyes closed, lips pursed like a small flower, and Blind Maklan staring into the fire. Dugas was leaning against a post, actually snoring even though he was on his feet.

Little Luki arrived, plucking at her skirt, as if it was made of itchy ivy.

Slowly the courtyard filled with children and mothers with their babies. We formed two orderly queues in front of the ancients, children on one side and mothers with babies on the other.

'Spirits!' Salluyud solemnly intoned. 'Protect our precious ones while their mothers work in the fields.'

I felt Luki's elbow in my side. She was smirking. *'Precious ones,'* she said quietly.

'They thought you were precious too when you were a baby,' I whispered, elbowing her back. 'Everyone knows better now.'

'Silence!' Maklan yelled, scowling in our direction.

One by one the women kissed their babies and surrendered them to the ancients. The ancients in turn distributed the infants to us waiting children like sticks of sugar cane.

If only they really were sticks of sugar cane.

Dugas picked up a baby with a big head covered with thick, bushy black hair. He beckoned to Luki. She accepted the baby, nose wrinkled, as if she was being handed an armful of water buffalo dung.

Pito held up Baby Baba, who was the size of a suckling pig. He staggered towards the queue of children and we all shrank back at the sight of the giant infant. Baby Baba was teething and he had tiny, sharp biting teeth. I prayed to Mother, *Please, grant me any baby but not Baby Baba!*

'Samkad!' Pito roared, dumping the huge infant into my arms.

'Ba-ba-ba!' Baby Baba cried joyfully, clamping his teeth into my shoulder. I felt something hot and wet sliding down my leg.

I held him away from me, his weight practically pulling my arms out of their sockets. His bottom ejected a small stream of yellow mush.

'Ha ha! Fertilizer!' Pito called. 'Well done, Baby Baba!'

'Ba-ba!' Baby Baba said.

There were two rice valleys. The first, nearest the village, was called First Valley. The second, just beyond the ridge, was called Second Valley, although everyone called it Second Best because the first valley was always first to be weeded, first to be tilled, first to be planted, first to be harvested.

First Valley was full of people shouting, singing, complaining and arguing as they worked the paddies. How was anyone supposed to put a baby to sleep? Luki and I headed to Second Valley, which was so quiet the babies we were minding spent most of the day asleep while we lolled around on a grassy embankment.

It took an age for us to work our way across – too many people with huge baskets of manure on their heads, marching up and down the steep embankments. We had to keep giving way, stepping off the path into the thigh-deep paddy water. Nobody asked us where we were going.

Up on the ridge that divided the two valleys, Tambul was standing guard. As we climbed up the tiers to the ridge, I shielded my eyes from the glare of the sun, trying to identify the small figure standing next to him.

I sighed. It was Bitteg, holding a spear that was double his height. No doubt the ancients had assigned Tambul to be Bitteg's mentor. It should have been me, I thought, willing my feet not to walk in the other direction.

Tambul greeted us with a shout.

'Hail, Samkad. And hail, Luki-in-a-skirt!'

Luki smirked. 'Hail, Tambul-in-the-tiniest-breechcloth-in-the-world!'

Tambul burst out laughing and Bitteg blushed as red as a radish, dropping his spear. He barely caught it before it splashed into the waters of the paddy below.

'Is that Baby Baba?' Tambul pointed at the baby on my hip. 'Respect! I swear every time I see Baba, he doubles in size!'

'Where are you going?' Bitteg said in a soft voice.

'Bitteg!' Tambul clicked his tongue. 'That's no way to be a guard. Be commanding. Demand an answer!'

Bitteg bit his lip and nodded.

'Go on, you know what to say.'

'Nobody's allowed into Second Best,' Bitteg mumbled.

'Why not?' I cried. 'We were allowed last year!'

'Because the ancients say so.' Tambul shrugged.

57

'But . . .' I began.

'We're not going to Second Best,' Luki interrupted.

Tambul raised an eyebrow.

'No,' Luki said. 'Actually we're here with an urgent message from the ancients.'

Tambul looked sceptical.

'Yes,' she continued. 'They want you.'

'I don't believe you.'

Luki shifted her bushy-haired baby on her hip and shrugged. 'That's the message. Salluyud looked so angry I thought he was going to explode. Isn't that right, Samkad?'

I tried not to grin. 'Uh huh. Salluyud was spitting like a cat.'

'You'd better hurry . . .' Luki began, but Tambul was already flying down the steps to the village trail.

'I'll be right back, Bitteg!' he called over his shoulder.

As soon as Tambul was beyond hearing, Luki whirled round and began climbing the last steps over the ridge.

'No! Nobody's allowed to enter Second Best today!' Bitteg cried in a squeaky voice.

Luki laughed. 'A little more practice and you'll get it right, Bitteg. Come on, Sam!'

'But but but . . .' Bitteg stammered, his forehead suddenly shiny with sweat. He lowered his spear to block my way, but its weight yanked him abruptly down. He tumbled head first into the rice paddy below with a loud splash.

Luki and I crossed the ridge into Second Best without a backward glance.

10

The First Valley had been shiny and neat, the paddies filled to the brim with water, and the stone embankments pristine – we'd been weeding them for weeks. But Second Best was a mess. Every gap between every stone in every embankment was hairy with weeds and the mud of the paddies were stubbled with cut stalks from the last harvest and matted with vines.

Our favourite spot in Second Best was a terrace just below the ridge that was so long and thin that nobody ever bothered planting it up. It was basically just a broad ledge covered with long grass. We spread out our blankets near the stone wall of the higher embankment and laid the babies, kicking happily, on top.

'Do you think they will roll off?' I mused.

'If we sit here, on the edge, we can stop them rolling off,' Luki replied. 'Even if they do roll off, the paddy below is just soft mud.'

'But there's so much manure down there!' I said, doubtfully.

Luki snorted. 'It won't make any difference to the babies. They already smell like poo!'

I peered deep into the cleft of the valley. Scrubby pine trees gathered at the bottom. I could hear the trickle of an unseen brook. There was a cave down there. The cave drilled deep into the bowels of the mountain and out the other side to the far end of the mossy forest. If the Mangili decided to attack, this was where the village was meant to flee.

There had only been one instance, since I began to remember, that we fled to the cave. I was no longer a baby, but not yet really a boy. I remember Father leading the way with me on his shoulders, and the ancients waving us past. Behind us, the other villagers trudged in slow procession. Up high on Father's shoulders, I kicked and cheered as we left them far behind, and were the first to enter the cave. The smoke from Father's torch puffed up to the cave ceiling and I squirmed with excitement at the sight of pointed stones, hundreds of them, thrusting out of the cave floor, like giant boar tusks.

We made our way down an endless stony corridor. It wound left and right and round and round until at last it opened onto a high-ceilinged cavern, with a bright green gash in the stone ahead. The gash was a fissure the height of four men, but only wide enough for one person to walk through at a time. And the green was the mossy forest beyond.

'This way.' Father was speaking softly as if he was afraid the trees would overhear him. 'This way.'

'Wait,' someone called behind us. 'Samkad. Stop.'

'Yes?' Father and I replied at the same time.

It was Father's friend, who was a little man, just a head and shoulders taller than me. Everyone called him Kacho, after the tiny sluggish fish that swam in the river. It took a lot of kacho to fill one belly.

'Samkad, my friend! It's all right!' He slapped Father on the back. 'No need to run now. The strangers are just traders. They're not dangerous.'

'Not dangerous?' Father repeated. I remember feeling a shiver in my belly at the quietness with which he said it.

'Truthfully, Samkad. They mean no harm,' said Kacho. 'The ancients have agreed to let them to stay. They sent me to tell everyone to go home. Many have already turned back. It is safe.'

Father nodded as if he agreed. But he picked me up and sat me on his shoulders, the tendons in his neck hard ridges under my legs.

Kacho continued. 'They don't speak our tongue, but they're very friendly. They gave us all a sweet drink from the lowlands. And rice cakes. Delicious.'

Father sighed, and when he spoke, his voice was careful. 'I think young Sam and I will stay here in the forest,' he said. 'We'll return when the strangers have gone. Will you let the ancients know?'

'But seriously, Samkad, they're not here to fight us,' Kacho insisted. 'My children loved their rice cakes and they have been respectful to my old parents.'

But Father would not be persuaded and we walked away from Kacho to set up camp and await the strangers' departure.

It was the dry season. I remember helping Father collect banana leaves to lay on top of a frame made of branches, to shelter us when we slept. I remember the faces of monkeys watching us from the trees. I remember Father catching a small gecko and tying a string around its neck so that I could play with it. I remember listening to its strange, loud cries of 'Took-oh! Took-oh!' I remember hoping that the strangers would never leave so that Father and I could hide in the forest forever.

Not many days passed before Tambul turned up, sent by the ancients to fetch us home.

I was so caught up with my gecko that I didn't even say hello. Nor did I notice the way his head drooped between his shoulders or how urgently he and Father whispered to each other.

'We must go home. Now.' Father's voice was hoarse.

I raged and stormed as he untied my gecko and let it scuttle into the bushes.

On the steep approach to the village, we began to hear a noise. It was the wind, moaning in the trees, I thought.

But it wasn't.

As we crested the ridge, we saw a procession of people amongst the houses.

They carried bundles wrapped in blankets. Six of them.

Father suddenly turned away and covered his face with his hands. 'Kacho,' I heard him sob. 'Kacho.'

I was only a child. A child does not think to say, well, why didn't Lumawig warn us? Why couldn't the portents just tell us exactly what we had to do to avoid danger? Why didn't the spirits drop a boulder on the heads of the strangers before they could do us harm?

The two strangers had beguiled people with gifts of sticky cakes and sweet drinks, speaking many kindly sounding words that nobody could understand. But they brought something deadly with them. Because within a few hours of their arrival, people began to die.

The first to die were those who most enthusiastically accepted their gifts: Kacho's family.

They all fell ill. Kacho. His wife. His two children. Both his old parents – who were the first to die.

By nightfall, Kacho's children were also dead. Kacho and his wife followed swiftly after.

As Kacho's family lay dying, the ancients, panicked and terrified, had the strangers marched to the House for Men. The old men ordered a small group of heavily armed young warriors to escort the strangers across several valleys, with their pony and all their goods. After they had walked two days, they bade the strangers keep walking. When the strangers looked confused, they struck them and chased them until they fled, taking their vile spirits with them.

But the problem was not like a boil that you could lance to remove its poisons. The damage had already been done.

Before the week was over, there were twenty more freshly dug graves in the village.

So Father had been right to stay in the forest. The ancients plied him with questions. 'Did a spirit whisper in your ear, Samkad? You were right to stay away . . . but how did you know to do that?'

Father just shrugged. 'I know nothing,' he said. 'All I know is what it's like to lose everything.'

From that time, no strangers were allowed to enter our village. When goods needed to be traded, the ancients selected a few people to leave the village. But the rest of us had to stay behind.

It was for our own good. Strangers meant danger and we were better off without them.

11

The day passed happily enough. We lazed on the grass and ate our packed lunches when the sun reached its zenith. We had to leave Second Best Valley to take the babies to their mothers to feed. Bitteg didn't bother to protest when we returned. He just rolled his eyes and let us through. He barely looked up when we returned.

Later, lying on our grassy verge and staring up at the wisps of cloud blowing across the sky, I wondered what Father was doing. Was he resting by the side of the trail somewhere, enjoying the sunshine?

Luki reached across, shook my elbow. 'Sam, get up. There is no time to waste. We should be planning how you're going to catch your Mangili.'

'No time to waste? Plan? We?' I groaned as I sat up. 'Since when was this about "we"? It's none of your business, Luki!

Besides, do you really think I can just stroll into the forest and capture a Mangili without getting my head chopped off?'

Luki ignored me. 'I don't think we have anything to worry about. We'll find one. My mother told me there are plenty of Mangili to catch. They are everywhere.'

'Your mother was just trying to scare you!'

'Scare me! Nobody scares me!'

'She's just trying to stop you going into the forest!'

'Mother says there have been many sightings.' Luki scowled. 'The Mangili live to hunt us, so why don't *we* hunt them? I'll bet there are some hiding in this valley right now.'

'There's nobody here but us!'

'But what if there was? What would you do if one turned up, huh? Are you going to run? Or are you going to fight?'

I opened my mouth to reply, but couldn't quite think of anything to say, so I shut it again.

Luki smirked. 'I knew it.'

I scowled. 'Knew what?'

'Everything you say is just buffalo dung, Samkad. You're just planning to sit on your heels and wait for someone to say, "It's time!" You've never been the type to go out and get what you want!'

'You take that back!' I shoved her in the chest.

For a moment Luki teetered, eyes round. And then she disappeared from view, landing on the terrace below us with a squelch.

I peered over the edge.

She was lying on her back, embedded in the slimy soup of manure and mud, with only the top slice of her body showing.

'UGH! UGH! UGH!' she screamed.

'Um, I didn't realize you were so close to the edge. Let me help you up,' I said meekly. I offered her my hand.

She peeled her arm out of the mud and slapped my hand away. 'UGH! UGH! UGH!' she cried again.

The bushy baby, as if sensing that Luki was in trouble, began to miaow like a little cat.

'The baby wants you?' I said in a small voice.

'SHUT UP!' Luki yelled, sitting up with an effort. The movement made her legs sink deeper into the mud. There was a tiny grey crab dangling from her hair.

'Oh look, a crab,' I mumbled.

She snatched the crab from her hair and threw it at me. It bounced off my chest and back into the paddy below.

Luki squelched to her feet, grasped the lip of the ledge and dragged herself up.

I backed away in case she was feeling vengeful enough to push me over the side.

But Luki ignored me, snatching up the bushy baby. She began to trudge up the steps leading to the next valley.

'Luki, come back!' I called.

She didn't reply. She just climbed up to the ridge and disappeared down the other side.

*

Glumly, I stared down at Baby Baba, gurgling and laughing on the blanket.

Why did Luki and I always end up fighting? I picked up a stone and, with all my strength, threw it deep into the empty valley. It made a thin splash as it disappeared beyond the firs at the bottom.

The sound cheered me up. I searched the terrace for more rocks. Soon I was pitching rock after rock down the mountain, enjoying the satisfying splashes as they landed in the invisible stream.

I checked on Baby Baba. He was fast asleep now, one arm out-flung, hand gathered in a fat fist, as if he had fallen asleep in the middle of trying to punch somebody.

I threw another stone, this time looping it high, high, high. I realized that I'd thrown it short when it peaked and began to drop, plummeting towards a paddy that was only midway down the mountain.

It fell into a wild clump of bamboo and shrubbery.

Was I imagining it or did one of the shrubs yelp in pain?

'Is anyone there?' I called.

The bamboo canes rattled against each other and the shrubs rustled.

'Stop!' I commanded, even though in my chest my heart had begun to pound. 'Who are you?'

With shaking fingers, I fumbled with my belt to free a sling I had made out of braided hide. 'Quickly, Samkad,' I panted as I began to fit a stone into the pad. I could hear Luki chanting,

Fight a war. Kill a wild boar. Kill a Mangili. I could almost see her mango face, nose in a twist, voice accusing: 'It's not just an opportunity. It's a gift! Are you going to do anything about it?'

I got the stone into the pad and I raised the sling to catapult it at the enemy. But the stone dropped to the ground and I had to refit it on the pad all over again. And then it was too late because when I looked up, there he was, standing in the paddy just below mine.

He was covered all over with thick grey sludge. He must have fallen into the paddy, like Luki. He had a small boulder in his hands which he lifted to throw at me.

The sludge split open to reveal a red mouth with white teeth.

'Rrrrrrrrrrraaaaaaaaah!' he roared as he threw the boulder.

But he was too far away and it was too heavy. It landed harmlessly in front of me.

I backed away, edging towards Baby Baba. I had to grab the baby and run. *Are you going to run? Or are you going to fight?*

But I couldn't run – my knees had turned to water and I crumpled to the ground.

The mud-covered Mangili quickly leaped up to my grassy ledge.

All I could do was throw myself at his legs. Wrapping my arms around his shins I managed to topple him over. But he was up again in a flash, grabbing me by the shoulders and slamming me painfully against the stone embankment behind us.

What did Tambul say about close combat? I thought frantically as I flailed about under my attacker's weight. Ram your

69

opponent with your forehead? No! He said something else.

Then I remembered. I could hear Tambul's voice, as if he was shouting in my ear. *Use your knee. Whack him in the groin.* I willed my knee to move. But it was impossible. I was pinned to the wall.

The stone knuckled painfully into my back as I tried to slide out from under him. And then his mouth opened wide. It took him a moment to release the scream, and when he did, I thought my ears would burst. His weight lifted.

I saw that Chuka had my enemy's ankle firmly gripped between her jaws.

I grabbed the Mangili's shoulders and with a quick, hard jerk, kneed him in the groin.

He howled, staggering backwards, hands clutching between his legs.

I gathered my right hand into a fist – correctly, the way Tambul always made me practise – and drew my arm back to hit him in the jaw.

He crumpled to the ground.

The unconscious creature was curled at my feet like a new baby, his hands tucked between his legs. My knuckles were throbbing now and i sucked on them to cool the pain. Chuka wriggled out from under the man and, turning her head sideways, slipped it under my hand. I smoothed her head and her eyes closed with pleasure. 'Good dog,' I whispered. 'Fierce dog.'

I had actually captured a Mangili.

12

A tingle thrilled up my spine. Here at last was proof that I could hold my own. Soon the ancients would be telling the story of Samkad, who overcame disappointment and showed the whole of Bontok what a real man was made of.

Weh. It was rich, Luki running off in a temper just when an actual Mangili turned up.

Baby Baba's great brown eyes stared up at me, mouth open, trying to decide whether or not to cry.

'Hush,' I said and miraculously Baba shut his mouth.

I dropped to my knees and rolled the Mangili onto his back. Chuka crept close, still growling inside her chest. I spat into my palm several times until it was wet – then I began to rub away the mud that caked his face. Clumps fell away to reveal thick black brows. The beginnings of a moustache on the upper lip. Black hair that fell over his forehead, but was cut around his ears and short in the back. Father had never mentioned that the Mangili cut their hair short.

It was a boyish face. He looked younger even than Tambul.

I wanted to see his tattoos. But when I scraped the mud off, there was only a narrow, brown chest. No tattoo. Not even a tiny caterpillar.

I sat back on my heels, disappointed. Didn't Father say you could tell how important a Mangili was to his community by how elaborately tattooed he was? This Mangili had nothing to show. The ancients would roar with laughter. *Captured a Mangili, Samkad? Was it worth even capturing this one?*

But what was he doing here, alone, in our valley? Or maybe . . . he *wasn't* alone. Maybe there were Mangili hiding all over Second Best, waiting for their chance to attack. Suddenly all the blood flowing inside me turned into icy river water.

I listened. I could hear the deep kaw kaw of a hornbill, the trill of crickets, the clicks and clacks of insects in the weeds . . . or perhaps it was a hidden army, signalling each other up and down the rice terraces? What if all this weedy mud suddenly cracked open to reveal bloodthirsty enemy warriors?

'Chuka,' I muttered. 'Can you smell anybody else here?'

But the dog had wandered several paddy fields below mine and was peeing on a random bush. No Mangili behind that bush then.

I relaxed. If there were strangers in the valley, surely Chuka would be barking her head off.

I dragged Baby Baba up onto my hip, and climbed to a

higher terrace. I should go now, get help, while the Mangili was still unconscious.

'That Bitteg is never going to be a warrior.' The voice punctured the silence so suddenly I almost lost my balance.

It was Luki, peering down at me from the high ridge with the bushy baby clamped to her hip. She had washed the mud from her hair even though the rest of her was still covered in it.

'What a mouse that Bitteg is. He just lets me in and out without a question. I have a mind to tell the ancients!' She frowned. 'What? Why are you looking at me like that?'

'Get help!' I yelled. 'There's a Mangili!'

'Eheh?' Luki hefted the baby and began to make her way down the stone steps. 'What are you talking about?'

'A Mangili! He attacked me! I—'

'Attacked you?' She looked doubtful.

'I fought him and—'

'Where? Where is he?'

'Over there, on the ledge.'

I turned to point at the unconscious stranger.

But there was nobody on the grassy verge. The Mangili had disappeared.

For a long moment, I stood there, opening and closing my mouth like a fish gasping in a net. How could I have turned my back on my prisoner? How could I have allowed him to escape?

'He was here! I swear it!'

73

Luki groaned. 'This is one of your stupid pranks, isn't it? You? Capture a Mangili single-handed? Do you take me for an idiot?'

'Yes,' I snapped. 'I definitely take you for an idiot ... because you don't believe me! He might attack again while you're sniggering!'

'Oh, shut up, Samkad. You must be really desperate to make up something stupid like this. There's nobody here.'

'WE'VE GOT TO GET HELP,' I roared. 'WE'VE GOT TO WARN EVERYBODY.'

Luki grinned. 'Sure! Let's warn the ancients that there's an invisible Mangili hiding in the valley! Then the men can come and search the valley armed with invisible spears.' She reached the grassy ledge and knelt right where the Mangili had lain. She began to untie the baby from her waist, talking to it the whole time. 'Are you hungry, baby? Don't worry, Samkad here will get an invisible mother to nurse you with her invisible milk!'

All around her the grass was trampled and flattened by my struggle with the Mangili. But of course, she didn't notice this, she was so determined not to believe me. I wanted to grab her by the shoulders and shake her until she listened.

It was only then I heard the barking.

'Listen. Do you hear that?' I said. 'Chuka's gone after him.'

'Gone after who?' Luki was still settling herself down on the grass.

I stared down the rice paddies, descending like steps carved

74

for a giant. Even though it was far away, Chuka's barking sounded desperate. It was coming from somewhere down below, where this mountain ended and the next one began.

Baby Baba squealed as I hoisted him high on my shoulder and set off.

'Where are you going?'

'Chuka's got the Mangili!' I yelled as I hurried down the stone steps.

'Wait for me,' Luki cried, gathering up the bushy baby.

I didn't think what I would do when I got there. Didn't think about how I was going to subdue the enemy with a huge baby over my shoulder. Didn't think that this wasn't a job for a scrawny boy but a proper warrior, with an axe to fight with. What did come to mind, as I picked my way down from paddy to paddy, was my dream. The one with the Tree of Bones, dripping with snakes, leaning into my open grave. Was this what the ancestors were warning me about? When I reached the foot of the mountain where the stream threaded its way between gawky pine trees and mossy boulders, I thought I could hear snakes hissing.

But it was just the soft rush of the water flowing into the cave.

And over it all, the barking continued from deep inside the cave's great black mouth.

13

Luki and I stepped into the cave and Chuka's barking was instantly thunderous, echo upon echo bouncing around in the hollows of the cavern so that it sounded like there were a thousand ferocious dogs waiting inside.

'We can't go in without a light,' Luki said. I rolled my eyes – I was already searching the ground outside for a stick with which to make a torch.

The pine trees at the bottom of the mountain were scraggly and scarred, seeping plenty of sticky pitch for burning. I needed a handle, but the twigs and branches that littered the ground were too dry and brittle. They would burn up faster than the pitch. I needed a greenish piece of wood that could stay unburned for a long while.

I put Baby Baba down on the stony ground and he burst out screaming.

'*Wah-wah-wah*!'

'*Bark-bark-bark*!'

I looked around wildly and grabbed a random stick with the barest tinge of green on it.

'*Wah-wah-wah*!'

'*Bark-bark-bark*!'

The noise made me clumsy as I scraped a lump of pitch off the nearest tree with the stick.

'Hurry up, Sam!' Luki called. She was clutching the bushy baby so tightly it was squeaking.

Laying the torch on the ground, I scraped up a handful of pine needles for tinder. I sprinkled the needles onto the pitch and began rubbing stones over them. Soon enough, one of the stones sparked and the tinder caught.

I felt Luki's breath hot on my shoulder as the torch burst into flames.

'Sam, you haven't got enough pitch!'

I was going to reply but then I realized that something was different. I could hear hollow echoing noises. The drip drip of water.

I could not hear any barking.

'Chuka!' I screamed, lugging Baby Baba onto my shoulder. The huge baby clawed at my neck, his weight almost pulling my arm out of its socket. I gritted my teeth and held him tight with one hand, snatching up the torch with the other. 'I'm coming!'

*

The air in the cave was a strange mixture – cold and clammy and warm a the same time.

The babies wailed as if they would never find comfort again. I realized guiltily that they were hungry for a feed. We should have taken them to their mothers ages ago.

But I sped up, jiggling Baby Baba on one arm while holding the torch high with the other. Luki cried out when a large gob of burning pitch dripped onto the stone floor, halving the brightness of the torch. 'It's not going to last! We should turn back!'

'No!' I snapped, hurrying forward in case she really did turn back. 'Chuka needs us!'

'But the torch!' Luki cried.

'Turn back if you wish,' I growled, though I knew that we had already travelled too far. There was only utter blackness behind us.

For all our haste, it was impossible to move quickly in the darkness. We groped our way, shouting for Chuka. But the dog did not reply. Instead the cave began to murmur, as if it was swearing under its breath.

'What's that?' Luki whispered.

There was an explosion of flapping and a cloud of bats flew over our heads, so low we could feel the brush of their wings and smell their odour. The floor of the cave, damp and slimy by turns, sucked on the soles of my feet. Baby Baba had stopped wailing to gnaw on my shoulder. He was hungry.

Our torch began to make a sizzling sound and more gobs

of fire dripped on the ground as the last of the resin burned away. Luki had turned silent. When I peered over my shoulder, she was staggering a little, the bushy baby fast asleep on her shoulder, tired out from crying.

The torch handle was burning in my hand and I clenched my teeth as I felt the wood scorching my fingers. I held on as long as I could, but soon dropped the torch.

It flared high and hot for a brief moment. I could see the tall arch of the cavern ceiling, the boulders that lined the path and the long tunnel up ahead.

And then it fizzled out.

We were in total darkness. It was black, black, black. So black that Baby Baba stopped gnawing on my shoulder. The air was thick and still. Heavy, like a blanket thrown over our heads. It was so thick it was hard to breathe through my nose. Like inhaling warm soup.

In the darkness, I had the strange feeling that everything around me was growing, slowly moving away. The cave walls were looming higher, the boulders stacked against them were expanding and the stone ceiling was rising. Up and up and up.

I was suddenly aware of a thousand tiny sounds. The distant drip of the stream. Bat flutters in faraway corners. And the rough in and out of our breathing.

I waited for Luki to blame me. *I told you, Samkad. I told you there wasn't enough pitch!*

But she didn't say a word.

I heard a small sniff.

'Are you crying, Luki?' I whispered. I was grateful that Luki couldn't see me in the blackness because the thought brought tears to my own eyes.

'Of course not – don't be stupid, Samkad,' she snapped. But she sniffed again.

'We're going to be all right, Luki.' I made myself say it like I really believed it. 'This passageway leads directly to the mossy forest on the other side. We just need to keep walking and it will take us out.'

Tentatively, I reached my hand in Luki's direction. My fingertips brushed against the wrinkly skin on the bend of her elbow. Her arm seemed to shrink from my touch.

'Luki, will you take my hand? So that we don't lose each other?'

I heard her fumbling, shifting the bushy baby to her other arm.

When my hand closed on hers, her fingertips were icy.

'Which way?' she whispered.

'This way,' I said, even though it was impossible to tell which way was what in the dark.

14

Father said if you stare hard into darkness, it will become embarrassed and melt away so that your eyes can begin to see. So I stared and stared as we trudged along. But the darkness only seemed to become even blacker.

A terrible doubt began to niggle in my belly. I remembered Father taking me into the cave that time when I was small. I remembered walking out of the other side, into the mossy forest. But what if I had got it wrong? What if this wasn't the same cave? What if these winding stone corridors led nowhere?

To my relief, both babies were asleep. Perhaps babies know when there's no point wanting something they cannot have.

Luki gave my hand an angry tug. 'We're in so much trouble,' she murmured. 'We've just walked into danger with two babies. The ancients are going to put us on kindling duty for the rest of our lives!'

If we are going to have any lives to live, I thought miserably. But aloud I replied, 'You didn't have to follow me into the cave, you know.'

'Of course I did,' Luki snapped. 'How were you supposed to do this on your own?'

'Did you come along to protect me then?' I said, bristling. 'What were you planning to do? Get that baby to pee on the Mangilis?'

'Shut up.'

'You shut up.'

I shifted Baby Baba higher on my hip and squeezed Luki's hand. The sound of our quarrelling was comforting as we crept blindly onward.

'Samkad!' Luki's fingernails dug into my palm. 'Did you hear that?'

I listened.

'You're imagining things.'

'I'm not! Can't you hear it? Someone's shouting in the distance!'

'What did they say?'

'If I knew I would have told you already.' She exhaled.

'Eheh,' I murmured. 'You begin hearing things and soon you'll be seeing monsters too. And then suddenly you find you've lost your mind.' But I looked around nervously. What if the ancestors of our enemies were lurking in the dark, waiting to trip us up?

The cold, musty air dug sharp fingernails into my back, tracing the tricklings of my sweat. There was a stink of decay.

I shuddered, wondering what dead things lay entombed in the rocks.

The blackness seemed to be thinning, though. I blinked, unsure if I was actually seeing the shapes looming ahead. I held my hand up. I could just see my fingers outlined in the murk.

'Sam, look!' Luki whispered.

I peered into the darkness. Was I imagining it? That vague, creeping light? That puff of air blowing against my face?

Luki pulled her hand from mine. 'Did you hear that?'

It was a voice carried on that tiny breeze – it was so distant the words had no shape. I couldn't even tell if it was a woman or a man.

Luki grabbed my elbow. 'Someone's waiting on the other side.'

'Come on, then,' I said. But I didn't move.

'We haven't heard Chuka for a long time. What if it's ... what if it's her killer?' Luki edged closer to me. 'What if that's your Mangili, calling his friends? We got this far only to lose our heads to the enemy! We should never have come!'

I swallowed. She was right. We had been foolish. We should've gone to get help instead of trying to rescue Chuka ourselves.

'What's that?' Luki whispered.

There was an odd scratching noise. Like someone was scraping a bone against the stone floor of the cave.

Scritch. Scritch. Scritch.

In the glimmer ahead, a small shadow detached itself from the stones. It began to move towards us.

I gasped. That scritching noise was just the sound of dog toenails against stone.

Suddenly, Chuka was leaping around us crazily, lapping tongue and scratchy claws and wagging tail.

'She's not dead!' Luki kept saying. 'She's not dead!'

No, not dead. But when I caressed Chuka's face, she yelped in pain. 'Are you hurt, girl?' I touched her face gently and she flinched. The Mangili had hurt her.

'Show us the way out, Chuka,' I breathed.

She whirled about and we followed. Almost immediately, the atmosphere in the cave changed, the air freshening. We turned a corner and there it was, the fissure that led into the forest. It was exactly as I remembered it. The bright green glow bleeding into the cave's darkness. Chuka barked an encouraging bark and slipped through.

I was about to follow when I felt Luki's hand on my arm.

'Is it safe?' she whispered. 'How do we know that the Mangili are not waiting outside?'

Chuka's head appeared in the fissure. She barked impatiently.

'Chuka wouldn't lead us into danger!' I said, shaking Luki's hand off and striding through the gap.

The green of the forest hurt my eyes. Long yellow shafts of sunlight bathed the forest floor. Everything was burning with life. I could see now that one of Chuka's eyes was half-shut and

I could make out a mottling on the black fur where she had been struck.

Little Luki staggered out of the cave, squinting in the bright light. The bushy baby stirred and she shifted it to her other hip. She tilted her head to one side, listening.

It was that voice again. We could hear now that it was a child's voice, speaking in a different tongue.

'Definitely not Bontok,' Luki said.

Chuka skittered around, barking and nipping my breech-cloth. She wanted us to follow. I bit my lip as we trudged after her into the trees. This part of the mossy forest was unfamiliar. I realized that my memory of the time Father and I had camped here was missing many parts. I did not remember the pockmarked stone leaning against one tree. Nor the giant banyan with a forest of aerial roots down to the ground.

Chuka led us to a pit, the kind used to trap boars. The long branches piled on top to conceal the opening had collapsed inward.

We peered in.

What was at the bottom of the pit was definitely not a boar.

It was a boy, skinny as the parched trees on the higher slopes. He was dressed in the most peculiar outfit I had ever seen. Dirty white cloth was sewn to the shape of his stick arms and stick legs.

He had a strange haircut, short, cropped closely to his head, around his ears and at his nape.

He planted his knuckles into his waist like someone

inspecting chickens in their cages and his face stretched into a big smile.

'Good evening,' he said, now speaking in perfect Bontok. 'Can you help me? I am looking for my brother, Samkad.'

Part Two
How to Know Nothing

15

The boy waited for us to reply, eyes moving from me to Luki, his foot tapping impatiently in the dried grass lining the boar pit.

'Do you know him? Do you know Samkad?' he demanded. 'You are Bontok, are you not?'

Was it me he was looking for? Could he be . . . I gazed down at his small, brown face, not daring to hope. At last some words managed to leave my throat. 'Samkad?' I mumbled. 'Which Samkad do you mean? From which village? There are many Samkads in Bontok.'

Somehow I couldn't ask him his name. I felt Luki's eyes on me. But she said nothing.

Baby Baba suddenly woke up. He panicked and grabbed my neck, clinging like an oversized monkey, his toenails digging painfully into my hip.

'Why are you dressed like that?' Luki said.

'Like what?' the boy replied.

'Like—' Luki waved at the muddy fabric that encased him all over '– that!'

The boy looked at himself and then at my breechcloth and Luki's skirt. 'Heh, I could ask you the same thing,' he smirked.

I turned to Luki. 'Can you take Baby Baba so I can help him out?'

'Do I have to?' Little Luki mumbled, even though she was already sitting herself on the ground and allowing me to drop Baby Baba on one knee while the bushy baby lolled sleepily on the other.

I selected a long branch from the pile covering the pit and slowly lowered one end into the hole. The boy grabbed it and, as I pulled, paddled his feet against the wall. He came up easily as a weed, the smell of boar urine and wet earth wafting up with him.

He stared at Luki and the babies struggling on her lap. Then he turned to me, smoothing his short hair and brushing clods of mud off his clothes.

'Thanks!' he said, thrusting his right hand out at me, fingers tight against each other, his thumb poking straight up.

It was so sudden I instinctively took a step back. Chuka stood on her hind legs and sniffed his fingers.

'You must shake my hand,' the boy said. 'It's what you do when you meet someone for the first time.'

He snatched my hand and shook it up then down, then up then down again, so violently that Chuka barked a warning. I wanted to snatch my hand away but all I could do was watch my hand as he jerked it about.

Then the boy turned and grabbed Luki's hand so suddenly that Baby Baba tumbled into the dirt.

'Ba! Ba!' Baby Baba squealed happily, wriggling onto his front.

I looked at my hand. 'Why did you do that?'

'Eh heh!' His chest puffed out and he peered down his broad nose at me. 'It is how AMERICANS greet each other!'

Luki scowled at him. 'What's an American?'

'Is that what you are?' I said. 'Are you an American?'

He gave us a patronizing look. 'Ahh. Of course. You people would not know about Americans!'

Before I could reply, Chuka slithered between my knees with a little yelp, then pelted towards the trees.

A man stood under the banyan tree.

Chuka scuttled towards him, fussing and leaping about like a fish. I stared, a great lump suddenly swelling in my throat.

'Father, Father!' I broke into a run, not caring that I was sobbing aloud.

Father flung his arms around me.

I revelled at the heat of his skin, the tightness of his arms, the soft sound of his heart beating against my ear. I was suddenly afraid Father would move away and I pulled him closer.

Father flinched, grunting in pain. I let go, staring at him with concern. He exhaled and smiled through gritted teeth, backing gently away from me to reveal a cloth bandage strapped around his middle. 'Don't worry,' he said. 'It's just a small injury.'

He gave me a reassuring smile. But I could see a welt fading on his cheekbone, dark shadows under his eyes, and a gaunt-ness that only comes from a long illness. 'What happened to you, Father?'

'I'm much better now, don't worry.'

He looked across at the boy we had just rescued. 'I see you've met Kinyo,' Father murmured.

The boy's eyes grew so wide they filled his face. '*You* are Samkad?'

Father smiled. 'Sam, this is . . .'

Kinyo gave a shrill whoop and threw his arms around me, picking me up easily with his twiggy arms to whirl me round. Chuka hopped about like an excited frog, her toenails catching on my leg.

'Samkad! My BROTHER!'

By the time Kinyo put me down, my head was spinning.

'You're Kinyo?' Luki was frowning.

Father looked at me. 'This is a long way from the village. What are you doing in this part of the forest with these babies?'

I felt like my head was full of river water. Here was Father. Here was Kinyo. The day had arrived. I was going to become a man at last. But if we told Father what had happened, if we told him there were Mangili about . . .

Luki looked across at me as she replied. 'We were minding the babies in Second Best when Sam ran into a—'

But before she could say 'Mangili', Chuka was barking madly again and the babies simultaneously burst into wailing and Kinyo was shouting, 'Quick, Aunt! This way! Look! Here is Samkad!'

A small woman hurried through the trees with a massive bundle balanced on her head. She looked just like any Bontok woman – face brown, cheeks decorated with tiny tattoos, hair dressed with beads, and skirt hanging down to her knees. But unlike a Bontok woman, her upper body was concealed under a top garment.

It could only be Agkus, Kinyo's aunt.

She threw her bundle on the ground and rushed towards us, smiling, her arms wide open. 'Samkad!'

But before she could throw her arms around me, Kinyo grabbed my hand and thrust it at her. 'Quick, shake hands!'

Laughing, Agkus shook my hand. I stared up at her face. I had always imagined a lined forehead and hair streaked with grey. But here she was, smooth-skinned, with shiny black hair falling over her forehead. The eyes were made darker by a thick fringe of lashes. She bent down immediately and picked Baby Baba up.

'Isn't he sweet?' she murmured.

'Ba ba!' Baby Baba gurgled.

She stared at the huge baby with a puzzled look on her face. 'Have the rules changed, Samkad?' she asked Father. 'I seem to remember that the ancients forbade children on this side of the forest.'

'Yes,' Father said, looking at me closely. 'You were just about to tell us, weren't you, Luki?'

Luki began. 'There was—'

'Let me!' I interrupted, tearing my hand away from Kinyo's grasp. 'We followed the dog into the cave, Father. We thought she was hurt.'

Luki's eyes widened. Out of the corner of my eye I saw her open her mouth, as if she was about to contradict me right there.

'We could hear her and we didn't think. We just entered the cave and the next thing we knew, we had emerged on this side of the mountain.'

Father bent to examine the dog. Chuka was immediately overcome with ecstasy at the unexpected attention. She flipped over onto her back, her eyes begging him to rub her belly.

'She looks like something struck her in the face,' Father said.

Kinyo bent to see. 'Look, a lump is forming above her eye.'

'We think she had an accident in the cave,' I said, glancing guiltily at Luki. Her mouth was still open, but her eyebrows had descended over her forehead into a deep scowl. Her glare demanded to know why I was lying. In my head, I tried to explain. I just wanted time, that was all. There was going to be a big fuss, wasn't there, when the ancients found out there was a Mangili in the valley. And my manhood would be over before it began. Again.

'But we can't be sure what exactly happened,' I continued. 'We didn't see.'

'Perhaps something fell on her,' Father said.

'Perhaps.' My voice was squeaky with guilt. I glanced at Luki again and my lies caught in my throat.

She was standing, the bushy baby, now lying in the ferns at her feet. Her face was rigid with horror, her fists clenched.

'Luki . . .' I stammered. 'I . . . I . . .'

She pointed. 'Monster!'

'What?'

'MONSTER!'

And I realized she wasn't pointing at me but at something in the wood, behind me. Something so huge its head was caught in the matted foliage of the trees, wringing water from the wet beards of moss and vines that throttled every branch. It was a giant, looming taller and taller as it struggled towards us, bending to avoid the grabbing trees. It was clothed in the same strange style of clothing as Kinyo, with a large hat made of straw on its head. As it lumbered forward a gust of wind blew the hat off to reveal a face that was the sickly white of buffalo milk. Instead of hair, the top of its head prickled all over with dirty yellow hog bristles, as did its chin and the top of its lip. Over its eyes hung eyebrows like a bird's nest, yellow, thick and tangled. Its nose was MASSIVE, speckled with orange spots, like the blemishes on overripe fruit. It had no lips. And its eyes!

95

They were eerie, alien things: bright and blue like the sky.

'Down, dog, down!' Kinyo plucked Chuka off the giant's leg. Then he turned to us, gesturing at the creature proudly.

'Meet my friend, Mister William,' he said. 'Mister William is an American. Shake his hand, Samkad!'

16

Mister William's enormous hand reached for mine.

'NO!' Suddenly Luki was between us, one shoulder dropped, head bent. She rammed into the American's knees like a little goat. The giant toppled over into the dirt, sending up a cloud of pine needles. Without a pause, Luki leaped on top of him, one knee on the vast chest, the other pressing into its pink throat, making its eyes bulge. The American made strangled noises as it tried to move her knee away, but she only pushed harder.

'He's not a monster!' Kinyo cried, grabbing Luki's arm. 'He's my friend.'

'LUKI! Stop it!' Father peeled Luki off Mister William as if he was removing a blood-sucking tick from a dog. He tossed her aside and bent to help the creature to its feet.

But Luki charged again, shouting, 'Monster! Monster!'

Father snatched Luki away. Her feet kicked in the air as he lifted her high.

The American coughed, clutching its neck, as it sat up. Under the bird's nest eyebrows, its blue eyes flicked from Luki to Kinyo. Its lipless mouth opened and it made a creaking noise.

Father pinned Luki's arms behind her back. She scowled, showing her teeth, tendons standing out in her neck and shoulders as she strained against Father.

'Little Luki,' Father soothed. 'The American is a man, not a monster. This is no way to welcome an honoured guest.'

An honoured guest? I thought, staring at the creature as it slowly rose to its feet. It looked nothing like any man I'd ever seen.

'What ignorant people you are! Of course he is a man!' Kinyo ran to Mister William and grabbed his arm. 'He's just tall. All Americans are tall.'

'All Americans are tall?' Luki stared up at the American. 'You mean, there are more of them?' The thought of there being more than one made me feel sick.

But Father smiled. 'He is just from somewhere else. He is called American after the place where he came from, America.'

'Where is that place?' Luki demanded. 'Where is America?'

Kinyo tugged on Mister William's arm. He opened his mouth and a stream of words I could not understand poured out. The American laughed. He understood! Kinyo could speak his words!

But now Mister William was looking at me, the corners of his mouth twitching in a faint smile. He pulled something out of a pocket at his hip and held it out to me.

I backed away.

'Take it! Take it!' Kinyo cried.

Reluctantly, I held my hand out, wincing a little as the American dropped something in my hand.

It was red. And sticky. And when I closed my fist over it, it felt like a small lump of clay from the bottom of the river.

'It's called a *gumdrop*!' Kinyo chortled. 'Taste it.'

The American's mouth was suddenly full of teeth. It took me a heartbeat to realize that the creature was smiling.

'Put it in your mouth!' Kinyo called.

Father and Agkus were smiling, and Kinyo was waving his hands about and Luki was watching to see what I would do. I popped it into my mouth. Almost immediately, its flavour began to burn into my tongue. It was sweet – but not the sweetness of fruit or of sugar cane. It was an intense sweetness that coated my teeth and my tongue. It was a sweetness so shocking I spat it into the bushes.

Kinyo looked disappointed. 'You're supposed to chew it.'

The American's great hand reached down and I recoiled. But he was only laying it on the top of my head. It was warm and strangely comforting. The sky-eyes blinked and he nodded at me, as if saying: no matter, everything is fine.

Father laughed, releasing Luki's arms at last and ruffling her hair.

'It's all right, children,' he said with a sigh. 'I'm just glad to be home.' He turned to collect the bundle that Agkus had thrown on the floor. Kinyo's aunt was on her knees now, crooning over the bushy baby, Baby Baba still in her arms.

Luki edged close to me, thrusting her elbow hard into my side.

'Ow!' I grunted, not daring to protest too loudly and attract Father's attention. 'Stop that.'

'What are you doing?' she whispered. 'Aren't you going to tell him about the Mangili?'

Kinyo leaned towards us.

I made my voice as small as I could. 'No. Not yet. Later maybe.'

'We should tell.' Luki glared at me fiercely. Kinyo was leaning out so much he was practically lying on the ground.

'Later!' I said again.

'Tell what?' Kinyo called.

Luki made a face at me. She turned to Kinyo. 'Who is he?' She nodded towards the American, who was watching us quietly.

But it was Father who replied. 'Mister William is our friend. He saved me from harm and—' Father touched the bandage on his side – 'he cared for me when I was injured. We asked him to come with us.'

'Yes,' Kinyo broke in. 'He had nowhere to go after our village burned down.'

I stared at Kinyo. 'Your village *burned down*?'

Father opened his mouth to say something but Kinyo just talked over him. 'Oh, we were going to leave anyway. My aunt thought it would be safer to stay in the mountains until the war is over.'

'The war?' Luki and I said at the same time. 'What war?'

17

The lowlands had always been a distant place to me. Who would want to go where there were no mountains? Not me. My life belonged here, in the highlands, here where our ancestors lived, here with my village, with my people. Anywhere else belonged to strangers that I didn't care to know.

But now? Curiosity burned in my belly. What had happened to Father? There was a weariness sloping his shoulders even as he insisted on hoisting Agkus's bundle up onto his head. His eyes seemed to flick everywhere, as if he was searching for hidden things behind every tree.

'What does Kinyo mean about the lowlanders being at war?' I asked as he led us along the edge of the mossy forest, following the line of the mountain. Chuka raced ahead. Luki plodded behind me with the bushy baby on her hip. I had reached for Baba but Kinyo's aunt was too enchanted by him and would not hand him back to me. Kinyo followed at her heels and the American trailed behind.

Father's feet slowed. 'They have been invaded by strangers who want the lowlands for their own.'

'Who are the invaders?' Luki had caught up with us. Her mango face peered at Father from behind the bushy baby's head. 'Who burned down Kinyo's village?'

Father glanced over his shoulder at Kinyo and Mister William.

'Why do you hesitate, Father?' I said.

'Samkad, I want you to understand that I owe Mister William my life . . .'

'What does that have to do with the burning of the village, Father?' I said, perplexed.

Father adjusted the bundle on his head.

Luki and I exchanged glances. Why was Father so reluctant to tell us?

At last, he allowed his gaze to meet ours.

'Americans,' he said. 'The village was burned down by Americans.'

It was so confusing.

How was it that we were walking amiably along with Mister William when his people were the very invaders that Kinyo and his aunt were fleeing? Why was Kinyo beaming up at Mister William like he was the most wonderful thing that had ever happened?

'He is our friend.' A quiet voice spoke up behind us. Agkus had been listening all along. 'He was our friend long before the invasion.'

Mister William had come to live in the village when Kinyo was just a toddler. Mister William had taken a liking to the boy, and perhaps he felt a little bit sorry for them too, because the lowlanders, just as the ancients had predicted, looked down on the woman and the boy from the mountains, and did not trouble to show them any kindness. The American was always kind to them, and over time taught Kinyo how to speak his tongue.

When Agkus's husband died, his family threw them out of their own hut, and Mister William took them in. When the Americans came and burned down the houses, their neighbours fled with no thought to warn them.

It was Mister William who came to get Agkus and Kinyo, who found a place for them to hide until the danger was past, who foraged for provisions and kept them safe.

No, Mister William was not an invader. He was a friend. Even if he was definitely an American.

When Father had set off to find Kinyo, I had imagined the journey would be fraught with axe-wielding Mangili waiting for a chance to take Father's head or vicious wild boar or unexpected cliffs to plummet from. But Father met no Mangili, and his journey was uneventful, even though it was long. It seemed to him the mountains would never dwindle, but then he climbed a final rise and at last saw vast stretches of flatter land spreading to the horizon. The lowlands.

There was a broad river at the foot of the final mountain and it was on its stony shore that Father built a fire to thank the ancestors for his safe passage. He crossed the river easily, the current just a trickle and the sun warm on his back. But when he climbed up onto the opposite bank, a strange unease came over him. He felt a vague chill, as if some of the cold river water had seeped into his veins.

The sun was beating down and Father was soon dry, even though a chill stayed inside him as he walked yet another day towards Kinyo's village.

The first sign that there was something wrong was long black threads of smoke curling lazily up into the sky. The second sign was a circle of large birds gliding in and out of the smoke. Carrion birds.

Father approached the village with every sense tingling, his spear at the ready, his eyes looking everywhere.

The village he had visited all those years ago had been a cluster of bamboo huts along a dirt road, each with a neat bamboo fence and a small garden of vegetables and fruit trees, with little shacks to keep chickens and livestock. The huts were surrounded by huge rice paddies – each capable of growing a hundred times more rice than any of our terraces in the mountains.

But now there was nobody to be seen tilling the fields. There were no children playing in the dirt. The village reeked with the smell of burning. It was a wasteland of ruined, smouldering huts, bamboo fences smashed and gardens trampled. Even the trees were on fire.

Father ran all the way to the hut where he had once handed baby Kinyo to Agkus and her husband. It was just like the others. A heap of wreckage, charred and slowly crumbling into ashes.

'Where is everybody?' he asked the dead house. 'What happened here?'

Then his arms were suddenly grabbed from behind, his spear wrenched from his fist. He was pinioned between two lowlanders, both roaring in their alien tongue as they wrestled him down to the ground.

One struck him such a blow across the face that for a moment his vision darkened and the smoking landscape was plunged into night.

The other lowlander held him steady with one hand and quickly jabbed Father's own spear into his side. Father pressed his hand over the wound, willing his soul not to leave him.

The lowlander drew the spear back for another thrust.

'Suddenly we heard a noise,' Father said. 'It was like a whole mountain had suddenly exploded. It was louder than the loudest thunder. And much more awful.'

The lowlanders had fled immediately, dropping Father's spear so that its long handle struck him in the face.

Father watched as they ran across the field. His hand over the spear wound was soaking with blood. His head felt detached from his body. Perhaps his soul had already seeped out into the dirt, he thought. He wanted to look down, to check, to see if it lay there in the wetness of blood gathering round him. But he found he was unable to do even that simple movement. And anyway, his vision had gone grey. He could barely see.

And then shadows appeared in the cloud. Voices exclaimed. Was that a man's voice or a child's? What were they saying?

Then . . .

'Samkad? Is that you?' A woman's voice, speaking in a language he understood. Despite all the time that had passed, he recognized it. Agkus. He'd found her!

He was lifted up and away and somehow, his soul clung on. He lived.

It was a gun that had made the noise, Father explained. And it was Mister William who had fired it.

The gun is a lethal weapon from America. It is like a spear in that you can kill your enemy from afar – but it is easy to miss with a spear. And if you miss, your enemy can pick it up and throw it back at you. But a gun ejects missiles called bullets that are deadlier than any spearhead, that can drill right through meat and bones to explode and kill you from inside your body.

After Mister William fired his gun and frightened away Father's attackers, the American carried him to the river where they camped until Father was well enough to travel.

Mister William had knowledge of healing. He cleaned Father's wound, sprinkling a stinging powder all over it before sewing the gash shut with a needle and thread. It was Mister William who had wrapped it in its bandage.

When Father peeled the dressing back to show us, I winced. It was a deep slice, the kind men suffer accidentally while butchering meat – the gravest kind of injury. No matter how the ancients pray and beg our ancestors for help, the scent of blood always draws wicked spirits like flies to carrion. It is they who make such lesions weep pus and putrefy so that the sufferer's soul flees his body, unable to bear the stink of rotting flesh.

Father's wound was clean, and the bandage was not yellow with pus. Clearly, the American knew powerful healing.

The moon waned and ripened in the time that it took them to make their way up the mountains. All that time, Mister William had tended Father's wound, cooling his fevers with mixtures that he produced from his pouch. And when Father became weak, he had carried Father on his back.

As Father told me the story, gratitude surged in my chest and I glanced over my shoulder at the American. I had feared him when I first set eyes on him. But he had saved my Father from the worst of fates.

Death is a gift – only the spirits can invite a soul to join the world of the dead, where life is eternal and the aches and pains of the physical world do not exist. When the ancients speak of death, their eyes glint with anticipation. Imagine, an eternal life without the cares of an aching back or a crumbling body! Imagine the mischief one could wreak upon one's enemies as an invisible spirit!

But only the spirits can lead a soul to the world of the dead. Accidents, illness, these are all the work of the spirits. Natural ways to die. But death by the hand of another man – or by your own hand – is unnatural and your soul becomes one of the Uninvited, banished from the world of the dead.

So Mister William had saved not just Father's life, but his soul.

18

We came to a swampy part of the forest, knotty tree roots scrawling in the dank, weedy wetness. We were suddenly wading, up to our calves in sludgy water, our feet skating on sliding mud. Father was so busy minding the bundle on his head that Luki and I soon left him and the others far behind.

'You didn't tell him! You didn't!' Luki hissed, her breath flattening the hair on the bushy baby's head.

I didn't answer. The truth was, I had not thought anything through. I left the Mangili out of my story not because I had a plan, but because Father was looking at me like I was the only thing in the world. If I had told Father about my encounter, he would have raced back to the village to alert the ancients, and then he would have been organizing the young warriors, rushing around the forest with their spears, hunting the enemy, while I stayed in the village to help the women pack bundles in case we had to flee to the caves.

'So are you going to tell him about the Mangili or shall I do it?' Luki whispered.

'Don't you dare. I was the one who fought the Mangili,' I whispered back, fiercely. '*I'll* tell him.'

'But when?'

We had reached firmer ground. I rubbed the mud off my feet with some grass and inspected my ankles for leeches. 'Maybe . . .' I mumbled, 'I'll tell him after the ancients give me the Cut?'

'Don't be stupid, Samkad. Nobody is safe until that Mangili is captured.' She shuddered, glancing around the trees dangling their moss over our heads. 'This is not a game. What if he attacks the village? What if people get killed?'

'All right, all right,' I mumbled. 'I'll tell him.'

'Tell him now.'

'Not right now.'

'When then?'

'Later.'

'What are you two whispering about over there?' Father caught up with us.

Luki made big eyes at me.

'Nothing,' I mumbled.

She scowled, but thankfully said nothing as the others caught up and Agkus handed me Baby Baba to carry, now that he had fallen asleep.

We walked on.

Tell him, Samkad, I told myself. *Luki is right. The ancients will need to know.* But every time the words began to leave my lips, I hesitated. Father would then have to leave me before he had even arrived. And how was I going to explain why I had not said anything?

At last we reached the beginning of the path that led to the village. I was miserable from hesitating. I had to do it now. The words were like a lump of rice choking my throat.

'Father, there's something important I have to tell you.'

He lowered Agkus's bundle to the ground and smiled at me. 'What is it, son?'

'In Second Best, I met a—' I began.

But Father was not listening. He shaded his eyes with one hand and looked up the path weaving through the green above us.

A crowd of people were hurrying down the mountain. There must have been twenty or more of them.

Father turned to Agkus. 'See! I told you that you will be welcome. They've seen us from the distance. They're excited and pleased that you have returned.'

But when the crowd came closer, all we saw were scowls and bared teeth. Their glares were searching, not for Agkus or Kinyo, but for Luki and me. There, leading the crowd, were the parents of Baby Baba and the bushy baby.

'WHERE HAVE YOU BEEN?' Baby Baba's mother screamed as she snatched him from my arms. 'Feeding time was ages ago. We've been searching for you everywhere!'

'Are you all right, my darling?' The bushy baby's mother wrestled him from Luki. 'You two are in such trouble.' And she gestured behind her where two young men trailed the throng, carrying Pito and Salluyud on their backs.

The two ancients were waving their sticks. 'Is it them? Are the babies all right?' they cried.

But even as the two mothers berated us for disappearing with their babies, the rest of the crowd suddenly turned towards Agkus, clustering around her like a cloud of bats. 'You're back! You're back!'

Then people had their arms around Father, clapping him on the back, and crying out in amazed voices as if they'd never believed that he would survive his mission. Kinyo was seized and spun round and round, his hair ruffled, his ears tweaked, everyone examining him closely as if he were some bizarrely shaped root someone had found in a paddy.

'He has his mother's eyes and his father's ears.'

'This lowlander hair will grow out quickly.'

'What big feet! He's going to be tall like his father!'

The scolding of the two mothers faded away as they realized what was happening around them. Soon, they too were crowding happily around Agkus.

I sighed with relief. Hopefully the new arrivals would distract everyone from the need to punish us.

Luki caught my eye – I followed the waggle of her eyebrows to the forest.

Mister William was hiding behind a tree.

113

I looked from the American to the noisy crowd welcoming the new arrivals. Mister William knew he would not receive the same welcome.

It was Father who revealed Mister William's hiding place.

'Where has the American gone?' Father cried. He spotted Mister William immediately and waved. 'Come, American. Show yourself to these people.'

Mister William's face turned a bright pink as he stepped out from behind the tree, his shoulders rounded as if he wanted to make himself smaller.

But there was nothing he could do to conceal his size. The sight of him made the women wrap their arms around their babies as if they thought he was about to swallow them in one mouthful. The men howled and rushed towards him, drawing their axes from their belts.

Tambul got to Mister William first. The American didn't resist, meekly allowing Tambul to shove him into the dirt. 'No! No!' Kinyo cried, struggling to free himself from someone's embrace. Tambul raised his axe and would have swiftly parted Mister William's head from his shoulders had Father not seized his wrist and twisted until he dropped it.

'What are you doing?' Tambul gasped.

But now here was Agkus, charging at Tambul. She pushed him away from the American . . . and suddenly it was Tambul who was on his back, and Agkus straddling him, slapping him so hard, it sounded like a log snapping in half.

'He's with me, Tambul, don't you dare kill him!' Agkus

cried. 'He's our guest! What kind of welcome is that! What is he going to think, after all the promises we made him—'

I was amazed to see a crooked grin spread slowly across Tambul's face under the bright red print of Agkus's slap.

'You remember my name?' he said softly.

Agkus slapped him again. But this one wasn't as hard a slap as the first – it barely made a sound.

Tambul swung himself to his feet, at the same time picking her up and holding her high above the ground by the armpits.

'Put me down, you brute!' she cried.

'Eh heh, it's nice to know you still remember,' Tambul said. 'I was barely a man when you left.' He lowered her gently to the ground before turning to the American.

Mister William had rolled up onto his knees, his blue eyes round, both hands high in the air.

By now, the ancients had dismounted from the backs of the young men. Old Salluyud shuffled forward. 'Who is this, Samkad?' he asked Father.

Pito was following close behind. 'You brought an American to Bontok?' Pito knew what an American was?

Mister William got to his feet, then, muttering something in his foreign tongue. His great hands slowly reached into his pocket and he showed his teeth as he tugged something out of his pocket. He held it out to Pito and Salluyud, head bowed.

Pito hesitated before he accepted it, turning it over in his hands. It was a slab of something, rectangular in shape and a cloudy blue colour.

'What is it?' Tambul said, peering over the heads of the two ancients.

'It's called a book,' Agkus said. 'It is precious.'

But Pito threw the book down. 'Does the American think such a trinket will win our trust?' He spat and several dark, wet spots appeared on the book's blue cover. He glared at Father. 'We don't want his kind here. We will have no part in their war.'

Luki and I exchanged glances. The ancients knew about the war!

Agkus put herself between the ancients and the American. She threw her shoulders back. 'With respect, old one, if this American comes to harm, *we* will come to harm. The Americans will punish us. You know that, I'm sure.'

'Ah, Agkus. It is good to see you again but I have to say, you are still as insolent as when we last saw you,' Pito grimaced.

'He is our friend!' Kinyo blurted out. 'Our very good friend.'

The ancients looked at Kinyo as if he'd suddenly turned into a stinky mound of dung in the middle of the path. Nobody spoke for a long moment.

Then the two old men began to shout questions at Mister William.

'Why are you really here?'

'Are the Americans going to attack us next?'

'Are you cracked in the head?' Salluyud shouted. 'Are you stupid? Are you a total idiot?'

Mister William stared at them, his white face uncomprehending.

Agkus wrung her hands. 'With respect, old ones, isn't it obvious to you that he does not speak our language?'

Father stepped forward. 'I beg you all to listen,' he said. And he told them what had happened when he arrived at the burning village, about the lowlanders attacking, and Mister William saving him.

'He did not have to do all the things he did to help me. He has a good soul. I trust him. And I believe you can trust him too.'

Salluyud opened his mouth to say something, but Father seized his hand and said in a firm voice, 'I will take responsibility for the American. I can vouch for him.'

Salluyud and Pito looked at each other, then Salluyud turned and put his hand on Father's shoulder. 'Samkad, you departed for the lowlands under the shadow of disgrace. But now, you have redeemed yourself. You have retrieved our beloved son and daughter from a dangerous situation, at great risk to your own life. We thank you.'

Pito nodded. 'The spirits of our ancestors have smiled upon you and brought you back safely. They would not have done so, if they did not have faith in you.'

Father gave a deep sigh and bowed his head. 'May the wrath of Lumawig fall upon my shoulders if I am wrong.' He turned to the crowd.

'Young Samkad!' he cried. 'Where are you, my son?'

I felt the urge to turn around and run away. But I felt hands on my back, propelling me forward.

Everyone began to laugh and chant. 'Sam-kad! Sam-kad! Sam-kad! Kinyo! Kinyo! Kinyo!'

Father stood me against Kinyo's shoulder.

'Tonight we will feast and celebrate!' Father bellowed. 'Our sister, Agkus, has returned with her nephew, Kinyo, who will become brother to my son, Samkad. Tomorrow, these two boys will be given the Cut and our village will be stronger by two men.'

19

How was I to speak to Father when all those people were shouting my name? Was I meant to hold a hand up and say, *Thank you, but hold the celebrations, there is something I must tell you?* Father was grinning, a thin sheen of sweat on his forehead, hand held high, nodding and accepting everyone's congratulations. I didn't want to spit on his joy. I couldn't just say, *Excuse me, Father, but there's a Mangili in the forest and we should stop being happy and sort him out before anything else.*

I watched, helpless, as everyone celebrated, beating their gangsas and shouting my name.

Deep in the crowd, I saw Luki's small face, straight-mouthed and grim.

When people finally began to ascend the trail to the village, the sun had begun to drop behind the mountain. A group of young warriors surrounded Mister William and escorted him up to the village.

Under the trees, Tambul was standing talking to Agkus, with his face so close, he was probably sprinkling her with spit. But she didn't push him away. Instead, she leaned towards him the way a whole field of rice leans towards the sun. 'Eheh!' someone called. 'Are you just a little bit distracted, young Tambul?'

When Father shouted that there were pots to boil and food to be prepared, Tambul and Agkus stared up at the trail, clogged with murmuring people.

Tambul ran up to me and grabbed my elbow. 'Samkad,' he said in a low voice. 'We are going to stay here a little bit longer. Tell the ancients I left my axe in the forest and we've gone to fetch it.'

'Why?' Kinyo said. 'Why are you two staying behind?'

But Tambul and Agkus had already turned their backs and were meandering into the moss-furred trees, his head bent low over hers.

'What does he think he's doing?' Kinyo muttered.

'I think he likes your aunt,' Luki said with a giggle.

Kinyo had a forlorn expression on his face. Was he upset about his aunt walking off with Tambul like that?

'You'll like Tambul . . .' I began.

But he shook his head. 'It's not that. What did your father mean by the Cut?'

'The Cut?' I frowned.

Kinyo blushed. 'When he said "the Cut" . . . did he mean . . . well, are they going to cut our foreskins?'

Luki smacked her forehead. 'Are you joking? Don't you know what the Cut is?'

Kinyo glared at her. 'Of course I know.' He looked around nervously.

'But aren't you looking forward to becoming a man?' I said. 'Isn't that why you returned?'

He shook his head violently, mouth scrunched up in horror. 'We came to escape the war. My aunt didn't say anything about my foreskin being cut!'

I stared at Kinyo with horror. He did not want to become a man?

He shoved Luki aside and leaned up close to my face. 'And another thing,' he said softly. 'My name is not Kinyo. It is . Antonio.'

What sort of name was Antonio? It was peculiar and foreign. The name of a stranger. I had looked at Kinyo and thought I was meeting my brother at last. But he was a stranger, an impostor pretending to be one of us.

I turned, half thinking I ought to race after Father, grab his elbow, warn him that there were strangers among us. But my knees were suddenly wobbly and I staggered like a just-born animal on spindly new legs. Sensing my distress, Chuka whimpered.

Luki grabbed my arm and held me steady. She glared at

Kinyo. 'Are you saying you're not really Kinyo?' she demanded.

'Hush, hush.' He looked furtively over his shoulder again at the crowd toiling up the hill behind us. 'Look, Kinyo was the name given to me when I was a babe. But of course when I was growing up in the lowlands, I had to take a lowland name. I would have been ridiculed if I'd used a Bontok name. I needed a name the lowlanders understood. So Agkus's husband gave me the name of his dead brother.' He shrugged, 'I don't mind if you'd rather call me Kinyo!' But there was a sour twist to his nose as if the name had a bad smell.

Luki frowned. 'But your aunt Agkus has not changed her name.'

He shook his head. 'Her lowland name is "Anita". I never heard her called "Agkus" until your father came along.'

Anita and Antonio. They were not to be trusted. And perhaps Mister William was not to be trusted too. Why did he allow his people to burn down the homes of his friends?

I took a deep breath, trying to soothe the chaos in my head. It made sense, I told myself. You cannot take your ancestors with you when you move away. People who moved to other villages always changed their names to that of an ancestor more local to their new home. That was what a name was for, wasn't it? To protect you.

Kinyo's face became pinched. 'Don't get me wrong, I'm grateful,' he said. 'Mountain folk are like dirt to lowlanders. No lowlander approved of my aunt marrying her husband and when he died, they couldn't wait to get rid of us.' He frowned.

122

'I'm glad to be here. But nobody told me anything about having my foreskin cut.'

I tried to breathe slowly. It wasn't his fault, I thought. It was the fault of his aunt, who didn't raise him correctly. She may have taught him to speak our tongue but there were other things he had to learn that were just as important. How could he have lived all his life without looking forward to his manhood? All the pride that had filled me when Father had named us both his sons trickled away like blood emptying from a wound.

He wrinkled his nose. 'Don't look like that.'

'Like what?' But I knew what I looked like.

We three were the last to reach the top of the mountain. Luki looked exhausted and Kinyo looked miserable. Disappointment weighed in my belly like a stone and my feet struggled to make purchase on the stony path. How had this happened? When Father had announced our manhood, I'd flushed with pride and relief . . . and sure, maybe I was a little bit anxious. But now . . . I was confused. My brother was not who I thought he was.

We walked into the courtyard. The House for Men shone in the leaping glow of the fire. It was night now and people cast long shadows as they bustled about, feeding the fire, hanging cauldrons, preparing for the feast. Small children ran about with the chickens, shouting gleefully, glad that the time for sleep had been delayed by the need to celebrate. It was a happy scene. But deep shadows quivered on the edges.

Father must have gone back to the house to change. He was

wearing his grand hornbill headdress again. Around his neck he wore crocodile teeth.

'Father!' I cried. 'Father!' I was trying to find the words to tell him about what I had just found out about Kinyo when I heard Mister William's voice, calling. He was towering over the ancients, who were sitting in their stone circle. He was speaking to Kinyo.

Kinyo just nodded, unsmiling, keeping his American words inside his throat as he sat down on the log.

Mister William smiled, as if Kinyo had greeted him warmly, then knelt on one knee and reached for something on the ground.

A strange sound emanated from the ancients' stone circle, a rough croak, like a toad in the muddy bottom of a rice paddy calling its brothers. Slowly, the croak sweetened to the quiet trill of a morning bird. And then the trill was chased by more bird-like sounds, high and low, all coming together in a single song.

It was a strange wondrous sound. Heads turned and the courtyard's happy bustle stilled. Even the children settled down and began to listen with wide eyes.

The sound was coming from a gleaming dark box on the ground. Attached to it was a handle that Mister William turned gently.

It didn't sound like anything I had ever heard before. Not the mournful wind moaning between the canes in a bamboo grove. Not the rhythm of the gangsas to which we danced during feasts. Not the sweet notes of a bamboo flute. It was a hundred bamboo flutes. It was a hundred melodies played together. It was a flowing, lilting, rushing stream that climbed high and then swung low. It was beautiful.

It brought such a strange aching to my breast that I pressed my palm against my chest to make the throbbing stop.

I looked round me. Every face gazed up at Mister William, eyes wide, mouths open and childlike. We were enchanted. It was as if everything that mattered had fallen away – there were no crops to worry about, no Mangili to fear, no invisible spirits to beware. The strange sounds made us free.

And when Mister William stopped turning the handle and the music ended there was a catch in my throat and a terrible sorrow had sprouted inside me like a vine that spread everywhere. I gazed upon the glimmering courtyard, the children, the men and women, the young warriors, the ancients. All that I had always known. And all that I could lose. Why had I delayed? I had to tell the ancients about the Mangili. We were in danger.

20

I lunged across the courtyard.

'Sam!' Father cried as I grabbed his wrists.

'Father,' I sobbed. 'I must tell you.'

The words hurried out of my throat as if they couldn't wait to be free. I told him what had happened in the valley. How the Mangili had suddenly appeared. How I had grappled with him and knocked him unconscious, only for him to vanish while my back was turned; I told him about how Luki and I marched in the endless darkness of the cave, the babies crying incessantly.

Father listened silently, but I could see the alarm creasing his face. When I finished, I looked fearfully at all the horror-struck faces around me, the mothers gathering their children to their breasts, the fathers reaching for their spears. Mister William looked around him in shock at our sudden transformation.

Father tore off his ceremonial finery, panting as if he'd been

126

running. 'I will gather all the men! Where is Tambul? He must command the warriors!' He snatched up a ladle of water from a clay jar and tossed it into his face to rouse himself.

Salluyud was scolding, 'Why did you wait until now to tell us? And to think we were going to make you a man, Samkad. You are a *CHILD. A FOOLISH CHILD!*'

'*TAMBUL!*' Father was bellowing now. 'Where is Tambul?'

'He and Agkus stayed behind in the forest,' Luki said. 'They said they would follow shortly.'

'I will get him,' Father said.

'No!' Salluyud cried. 'You need to organize the men. Now.'

'We'll do it,' I said in a small voice.

'You!' Father glared. 'You are children.'

'He can't be far away – we only just saw him leave,' Luki said. 'Anyway, there are three of us.'

'Fetch him, then. *GO!*' Father cried. 'I will follow as soon as I've got the men together.'

I snatched up a torch and Luki, Kinyo and I sprinted towards the forest path. Mister William lumbered after us, calling in his alien language. But we didn't stop to explain.

21

'I'll tell him. I was the one who fought the Mangili.' Luki mimicked me as we ran along. 'But no, you kept putting it off!'

'There wasn't a good moment—'

'A GOOD MOMENT?' Luki cried. 'There wasn't a good moment to tell them the whole village was in *DANGER?*'

'Oh, shut up, Luki!' But she was right, of course, I thought with a pang. Call myself a man? What kind of man would put himself before his village?

'Wait for me!' Kinyo was picking his way down the slope. Chuka followed behind, her head tilted to one side as if puzzled by his clumsiness. I sighed. My brother walked down the mountain like the lowlander that he was.

'I was an idiot to wait for you to tell them!' Luki fumed. 'I should have told your father myself!'

'Shut up, shut up, shut up!' I clapped my hands over my ears.

Kinyo caught up with us. 'But you said it was only *one* Mangili.'

'One is enough,' Luki said.

'What's so important about the Mangili anyway?' Kinyo bleated. 'Why is everybody so upset?'

'They are our blood enemy,' I growled. 'We have been at war with the Mangili since before we began to remember.'

'How can you be at war since before you began to remember?' Kinyo said. 'If you don't remember then how can you know?'

Luki glared at him over her shoulder. 'They attack us, we attack them.'

'You people make any excuse to chop someone's head off!' Kinyo declared.

'You people?' I sputtered.

'*WE ARE NOT "YOU PEOPLE"!*' Luki stopped and shoved Kinyo so hard in the chest that he almost rolled all the way down the hill. '*YOU ARE ONE OF US NOW.*'

'No I'm not! I just got here!' Kinyo cried.

'Pah!' I sneered. 'What you really want is to become an *American*! I see it in your face every time you gaze at that Mister William!'

'Mister William is my friend!'

'How can you be friends with the enemy of the lowlanders?' Luki snapped.

'But he's not like other Americans!' Kinyo protested. 'He's different!'

I stared glumly at the mossy forest below us as they argued. Before Father killed the snake, I knew the world I lived in. I knew that I would become a man, that I would have a family, that I would hunt and fish and plant rice. Now? I didn't recognize this world of war and tongues that spoke words that meant nothing to me.

The sky was alight with spiralling stars, but down below us the waiting forest was black, black, black.

Chuka, who'd raced ahead, stopped so suddenly I almost dropped the torch. She pointed her nose high in the air, sniffing.

'Get out of my way, Chuka,' I cried, nudging her solid body with my foot.

Chuka gave a deep growl and bolted down the rest of the hill, disappearing into the forest's black throat.

'Maybe she smelled a squirrel. Or a monkey,' Luki said.

'The monkeys are all asleep,' I muttered.

'It's so dark.' Kinyo's voice sounded a little panicky. 'Can you see anything at all?'

'Of course I can see,' I said, even though the torch was barely illuminating the trail in front of us.

'Well, *I* can't see,' Kinyo bleated. 'I can't see anything at all.'

'Why don't you turn back?' I muttered. 'You might fall into a boar pit again. In this darkness you will probably break your neck.'

'There's a pit?' Kinyo cried.

'Here, take my hand, Kinyo,' Luki said. 'Ignore Sam, he's a liar!'

'Thanks,' Kinyo whispered.

It was so annoying, knowing that, behind me, the two of them were walking hand in hand. I felt like turning round, and grabbing their wrists and yanking their hands apart. But I just walked faster into the forest.

Once we were under the trees, the atmosphere thickened, wrapping around us like a moist blanket. I could hear Chuka barking deep in the wood.

'Tambul? Agkus?' Luki began to call. 'Tambul, where are you?'

'TAMBUL!' Kinyo and I joined in.

I could feel the cold trickling through my veins, worming its way up to my chest and twining round my heart. I was suddenly glad for the darkness: Luki couldn't see that I was shivering, and not just because it was cold.

'We should have taken *two* of the torches,' Kinyo said.

'Don't be a baby. We're almost there,' Luki said. 'Can't you smell that? Wood smoke!'

I was relieved to smell it. Tambul and Agkus must have built a fire.

'Tambul!' I called. 'The ancients want you!'

'Tambul!' Luki cried.

I had the weird sensation that the air was undulating. *It's just fog*, I told myself, trying not to think of spirits watching from the trees.

I made myself walk on, ignoring the tiny scampering noises in the purple shadows and the heavy creak of trees in the wind.

131

Wet beards of moss dripped on the torch, making it sputter and spark.

A distant scream.

'What was that?' Kinyo whispered.

'Oh, you baby!' Luki said scornfully.

'It was just a monkey,' I laughed. 'Are you *scared*, Kin—?'

The taunt withered in my throat. Because we could all hear it now. Feet running in the shrubbery ahead. The torch sizzled and then its fire went out. Something exploded in the shadows, and someone was suddenly on top of me. Fingers were tearing at my throat, sharp nails gouged at my flesh. Sweat was flicking everywhere. Claws. Knees.

'What?' I heard Luki cry. 'What's going on?'

Now I was on my back I could see a tiny gap in the forest canopy, a triangle of moonlight above us. The torch guttered on the edge of my vision. The shadowy figure turned. I could see my assailant.

It was Agkus.

'It's me! It's Samkad!' I cried. 'Let me go!'

'Samkad! Oh, Samkad.' She was sobbing. 'The Mangili killed him. They killed Tambul.'

22

I don't know what I thought. Maybe I thought I could save him somehow. Maybe I wanted to prove that it wasn't true – that Tambul had not been killed, that Tambul was still alive.

I stumbled to my feet.

'No!' Agkus screamed. 'They might still be there!'

But I was running through the trees. Quickly. Quickly. I could hear the crackle and pop of a fire somewhere. There, on the other side of a boulder. A clearing. The fire was small, right in the middle.

Under the smell of wood smoke, there was another odour. What was it? It smelled like . . .

I knew the smell of freshly butchered meat.

There was an axe lying on the path. Tambul's axe.

There was a black shape sprawled across the trail.

A carcass with an arm, stretched out. A very human arm. Not just a carcass. A man.

I knew from the beginning who the headless body on the ground was. Even in the dim light, I knew those strong limbs. The deep chest. The pattern of gecko tattoos that marched from shoulder to breast.

I knew.

But the words that came to my lips were, 'Who is it?'

Whoisitwhoisitwhoisitwhoisitwhoisit?

And then I was screaming his name.

'*TAMBUL!*'

An icy fist wrapped itself around my heart and squeezed, stopping the life inside me. I could not breathe.

Then I found myself on my knees, arms outstretched. I wanted to gather Tambul up in my arms. But the gaping wound where his head had been filled me with terror. When I gingerly lowered my palm to the broad chest, I could feel the soft heat swiftly dissipating, turning the warm, living flesh into cold, unyielding meat. I snatched my hands away and stumbled to my feet, wanting to flee.

My knees were dripping.

Blood.

I could smell it as it trickled down my leg, oozing into everything, coating every pebble, spilling out over the dirt, seeping between every blade of grass, spreading deep into the ground, soaking into roots of the trees, into the ground, into the caverns below, filling the mountain.

Blood.

White threads of mist were pooling around the body, submerging Tambul slowly.

And then Luki was there. Her arms were around me. Her wet cheeks pressed against mine. Her lips were moving, but I was deaf. I couldn't hear her.

My windpipe opened and though I knew that screams were leaving my throat, I heard nothing.

Luki shook me and, slowly, sounds began to filter into my hearing. The *scratch-scratch* of the small fire. The wind whistling in the trees. The sobs of the others.

Agkus was a vague shadow away in the trees. When she spoke, she sounded broken. 'We were sitting by the fire and the Mangili dropped down from the trees. Two of them. Tambul tried to fight, but they ran him through with a spear. I fled and then I thought they had caught up with me. I fought. But it was you.'

Kinyo ran to his aunt and clutched at her elbow. 'Aunt, come, let us go back to the village! Please, let us go back now.'

She nodded. 'Yes. Yes. We must. What if there are more of them?'

More of them.

There had only been one this morning.

And now there were two.

If I had told the ancients earlier, if I had spoken up, this would not have happened.

135

Tambul was dead. The village was in grave danger. And it was all my fault.

23

'Hurry,' Agkus gasped, as we turned to leave. 'Hurry.'

Eddies of mist suddenly appeared, gleaming gold in the light cast by the fire as it wound round our knees. Shadows huddled over us in the trees. We glanced fearfully around us, but if our enemy was hiding somewhere in the forest, it was impossible to see in the darkness. Were the Mangili watching us now from some secret hiding place? Were they amused by our despair?

The forest air was suddenly filled with many shouting voices and the mist parted to reveal Father and torches and spears and five other grim-faced men, gaping at the corpse in the clearing.

'How long ago?' Father's voice was harsh. Agkus mumbled an answer and Father nodded. 'We must move quickly.' He sent three of the men into the trees to search for the murderers. The other two hacked a great pole of bamboo from a thicket and lashed Tambul's poor headless body to it. They carried him home, dangling on a pole like a freshly-hunted deer.

The trail was wet, the moss sucking on our feet as we made our way up to the village. Agkus was hopeless, needing Father's support to put one foot in front of the other.

When we reached the skull pillar at the top of the hill, Father gave a signal and the men lowered Tambul to the ground. One began to fix torches to the gate and the other ran to the House for Men to tell the ancients what had happened.

'Wood!' Father commanded. 'Bring wood to build Tambul's funeral chair.'

'Build the chair? Here, outside the village?' Agkus cried, as the rest of the men scattered to gather wood.

'Tambul cannot enter the village,' Father said quietly. 'You know why, Agkus.'

'No!' Agkus threw herself at Father, clutching his arms like a drowning woman. 'Don't leave him out here alone!'

Father gently took her hands in his. 'This is the way it has to be,' he said. 'Tambul died an unnatural death. The spirits will not have him in the village. He is one of the Uninvited now.'

People were coming to the gate. I could hear their shocked whispers. *It's Tambul! The Mangili took his head.* 'Tambul!' someone shouted, far away. 'Tambul!'

'We will honour him,' Father said softly. 'We will build him a death chair. We will sit with him. He may have died an unnatural death, but he is still our own.'

Agkus seemed to waver – she would have fallen to the ground if there had not been several women nearby, who caught her, throwing their arms around her and lifting her up.

'The ancients have ordered everyone to the cave,' one of them said. 'Most people are already on their way. We will take her there.' They led her away. Agkus didn't resist, her body spiritless and limp.

A tall shadow unfolded itself from under a tree.

'Mister William!' Kinyo cried, running and throwing his arms around the American's waist. Despite the dozen torches flickering on the fence, Mister William's face remained in shadow.

The ancients were shouting before they stepped out of the village, praying loudly to our ancestors, begging them to protect us from the Mangili.

Where is your spirit now, Tambul? I wondered. *Are you in the shadows, watching in bewilderment as Father carefully builds a high backed chair out of the wood we gathered? Are you horrified to see us lift your corpse so clumsily? Do you mind that we are sitting your dead body in the chair, crossing the ropes across your chest, and tying your ankles to the legs with your feet resting on a footrest of bamboo?*

I arranged Tambul's hands carefully on his knees – they were heavy, the skin dry like bark. His fingernails had turned purple. Salluyud brought a white shawl adorned with spirit symbols to drape over the gaping wound where Tambul's head had once been. Over this, Pito hung ceremonial strings of boar tusks and dog teeth.

In the firelight, Tambul's skin had darkened to charcoal. It was icy to touch. The headless figure looked small in the high-backed chair.

'Children,' Father commanded. 'Go now. Join the others in the cave. Luki, your mother is waiting for you there. Take the American with you. It will be safer there, in case the Mangili are planning to follow this with an attack on the village.'

'But they've already killed Tambul!' I cried. 'Why would they attack again?'

'Go. Now,' Father said firmly, turning his back on us.

We obeyed.

Kinyo called to Mister William, translating Father's words. The American collected his bag from under a tree and strapped it onto his shoulders.

'Which way?' Kinyo said.

'Just follow everyone,' I murmured. 'Look.'

From where we stood, we could see the flickering dots created by the torches of people making their way to the cave on the black shadow of the mountain ahead. The distant wail of a baby echoed in the valley. Just ahead of us a man put a small pig on his shoulders.

'I don't want to go back into that cave,' Luki whispered.

I shrugged my shoulders, staring up at the moving dots of light on the black mountain.

'I'm just going to get a blanket,' I said suddenly. 'You go ahead. I'll catch up.'

'All right,' Kinyo said, moving ahead with Mister William.

But Luki stayed, glaring at me. 'Why do you need a blanket?'

I didn't answer.

'Weh.' Luki stamped her foot on the ground. 'I know you, Samkad. You're going to stay, aren't you?'

I sighed. 'Tambul would want me to stay. If *you* were dead wouldn't you want your friends to sit with you?'

Luki looked at me for a heartbeat.

Then her foot lashed out, striking my ankle.

'Ow!' I yelled. 'What was that for?'

'I'm staying too,' she said. 'He was my friend just as much as he was yours.'

We fetched our blankets and crept back to Tambul's death chair. The ancients had taken up positions round it, sitting on their heels with their chins tucked into their chests. They were asleep. On the ground someone had already laid a bowl of rice wine as an offering to any spirits who might wander by. There were two guards leaning on their spears. But they made no move to stop us as Luki and I crept into the shadow of a boulder not far from the tree fern pillar. We spread our blankets out and lay down. Chuka whimpered and slithered into my arms, her hot doggy breath blowing into my neck, the warm, furry body pressed against my belly, the wagging tail flicking against my leg.

Soon the tail grew still, Chuka began to snore, and I began to dream.

24

I was dancing.

My arms were raised like eagle's wings; my feet were moving to the rhythm of the gangsas.

I knew I was dreaming because leaping about around me in a silent dance were men, women and children made of shadows.

I wanted to stop but I couldn't. My feet kicked and my arms waved as I threaded in and out of the dancing shadow figures. I could not stop. It seemed as if I was cursed.

Suddenly, a gusting wind. It pushed under my outstretched arms, lifting me up, up, up in the air. Higher and higher so that down below, the shadows shrank to black smudges round the fire's red flower. The trees that had towered over me on the ground dwindled into green buds and clumps.

I rose fast and high.

Far below, the rice terraces were green glinting tiers. The forest wrapped its wet dark skirts around the mountain's waist.

I rose swiftly.

Up and up. Now I was in the clouds, which were great white mountains, high cliffs, white forests, white slopes of floating scree.

Beyond, there was a blue ceiling. I couldn't tell if I was rising towards it or if it was dropping down. I closed my eyes. Bit my teeth together. Waited for the splintering when I crashed through it. It didn't splinter. It was elastic, like the pig's bladders we filled with water on butchering day to throw around.

The wind pushed under me and the sky pushed down. Such a funny sensation, pressing one's head against the sky. Then, *pop*! The sky split and my shoulders squeezed through the small opening. I burst out on the other side, laughing.

But my exhilaration swiftly turned to fear.

Because beyond the sky's blue skin was a world not meant for the living. This was the home of the Uninvited. I fought the wind. I wanted to get out, go home. But the wind wouldn't have it. It blew harder, spinning me over and over and on and on.

There was no sun. Below me were rows of black-barked trees with writhing black branches and fluttering black canopies. They formed the edges of great black paddy fields where hundreds of shadowy figures waded, waist-deep in black, waving grain. The figures looked human ... but instead of heads, dark flames guttered from their necks. They burned with a strange fire, that became darker the higher the flames roared.

The wind made a loud gusting noise. The heads of black flame lifted. In each burning face the mouths were deeper, blacker smudges that opened and closed. They were calling. But I heard nothing.

The wind suddenly turned and began to press me down. The black fields rose to meet me.

No! I tried to stop my fall by flapping my arms like a bird. To no avail.

The eyeless creatures below swivelled as one, somehow following my descent. As one, they raised their arms towards me. I could see them clearly now. Not just their flame heads but their bodies . . . bodies of dead men and women in various states of ruin – slashed, broken, torn, peeling skin, broken bones. These were people who had met their deaths through war and murder.

Down, down, down. My feet touched the ground and the Uninvited began to move, the silent black shadow-mouths constantly moving, arms still outstretched. The black waters of their rice paddies made every movement slow and laboured.

But then I heard a swift thud-thud-thud. Running feet. One of the creatures had suddenly darted out of a paddy onto an embankment. He was racing towards me.

Not for him the achingly ponderous movements of the others. I could see that this spectre's body was young, lithe and undamaged.

144

Just before he raised his axe, I recognized the tattoos across his chest. Geckos.

The shadow mouth howled silently in the head of flames.

I begged Tambul to stop.

But it was too late because he was hard upon me, his blade swinging. As it cleaved my neck open, a scream was freed from my throat.

25

'Samkad! Samkad!' Luki sounded frantic. 'Samkad, wake up!'

But I couldn't. There was an invisible boulder pressing down on my chest, crushing the cage of my bones, squeezing the air from my lungs, pinning my wriggling heart to my spine.

'Sam!' I realized that Luki was not the only one shouting. I could hear Chuka barking and the bellowing of men and ancients.

'Come on, Sam! Wake up!'

I willed my hand to move, but my hand would not obey. I felt the cold trickle of sweat down my nose. Father had told me about this. How spirits could immobilize you. And if you couldn't rouse yourself, you could die, right in the middle of your dream.

'WAKE UP!'

The boulder rolled off me at last and air rushed into my

chest. My heart, unpinned, began to beat again, and I hastily propped myself up on one elbow.

'There!' Luki pointed down the path to the mossy forest.

I rubbed my eyes. Tambul still sat, stoic and headless, in front of the gate. The morning was not yet fully ripe. The sun was nowhere to be seen even though the sky was already warming to a vague light. Around us, men and ancients pointed and stared down the mountain.

Wading through deep pools of mist, three strange creatures ascended towards us.

They had great, waggling heads and legs like tree trunks. The mist billowed and gathered around them like a ghostly river and a scent, ripe and beasty, wafted on the breeze.

'What are they?' Luki whispered, huddling against me. I was still in the grip of my dreaming and it took me a while to tell myself what the creatures were. Were they the souls of long dead beasts come to visit us? Or were they perhaps boulders from a neighbouring mountain that had come to seek somewhere else to lie?

Horses. That's what they were.

I'd only ever seen a horse once, when I was still small, when one wandered into the village, trotting between the houses. I remember thinking what a strange animal it was. I remember everyone shouting and running. Several men blocked its way. They tried to throw a rope round its neck. But it swung round and galloped down the mountain and we never saw it again.

147

It was only when the horses clop-clopped up onto level ground, snorting and making shrill noises in their throats, that I looked at the men sitting astride them. I could tell they were tall, and not just because they sat high above us. They were dressed like Mister William, except the fabric that wrapped round their limbs was coloured blue. Bands of black hide crossed over their chests and round their waists. Their legs were sheathed to the knee in dirt-coloured wrappings, their feet encased in even more black hide. Hats shielded their faces.

The ancients behind us muttered to each other. I couldn't make out what they were saying, apart from one word. Americans.

I pressed my lips together to stop my jaw dropping open. Until yesterday, I had never met anyone from outside our village, never even heard of Americans. And now . . .

Father was suddenly there. He had a spear in one hand and he stood it firmly in the ground at his side, his feet apart, shoulders square, his other hand on the axe hanging at his waist. 'What do you want?' he demanded, his voice hard.

One of the riders lifted the hat from his face and I felt the same shock from the other day when I saw Mister William for the first time. This American had the same pale skin, the same strange blue eyes. On top of his lip, he had a fat roll of moustache that curved down the flanks of his jaw.

The American's voice began to roll out of his chest, deeper than any male voice I'd heard before. He spoke many words, a long stream of incomprehensible sounds, and the corners of Father's mouth drooped in disappointment.

The American looked impatient and said something else, his voice louder this time.

'The idiot American thinks he only has to raise his voice to be understood,' Salluyud snorted.

'With respect, old one,' Father said in a low voice, 'we must try not to offend them.'

'Pah! He can't understand a word I say, can he?'

'We need the boy, Kinyo, to speak for us,' Father said. 'Someone must fetch him from the cave.'

Salluyud signalled one of the younger warriors to go. As the man hurried off, he called, 'Bring the other American too.'

The American with the moustache bent over his horse's head, fixing his blue gaze on Salluyud.

To my surprise the ancient bowed his head and ceased to speak.

Just then the two Americans who, until now, had been sitting silently on either side of the moustache, cried out. They swung their long legs over their horses and dismounted, chattering excitedly as they pushed past Father.

'They want to look at Tambul,' Luki whispered.

The moustache hopped off his horse and hurried to join them as they approached Tambul's seated corpse.

'Disrespect!' Dugas cried.

But, of course, the Americans didn't understand. They just glanced at Dugas and bared their huge white teeth. One of them turned and lifted up the spirit blanket to examine the gash where his head had been.

I heard sharp intakes of breath behind me and I glanced worriedly at the younger warriors. They were Tambul's friends. Were they going to draw their axes and fall upon the Americans? Their eyes darted about, following the Americans as they moved slowly around the death chair, exclaiming to each other. But they did not move.

Dugas sighed. 'Samkad,' he called to Father in a low voice. 'Are these Americans here because of you? Do you think they followed you here from the lowlands?'

Father shook his head. 'I do not think anyone followed us, old one. I cannot know why these Americans are here until Kinyo arrives to ask them.'

Muddo, who was Tambul's closest friend, turned to the others. 'There are only a few of them! What are we waiting for? With our numbers we can overpower them.'

'Muddo.' Father spoke quietly even though there was no chance the Americans would understand. 'We kill one American today and there will be a hundred more wanting their vengeance.'

A hundred more! My mouth went dry.

Muddo clamped his lips together and frowned at his toes.

Now the American with the moustache ran back to his horse and fetched a bag from a pack slung over the creature's rump. He took it back to the death chair and from out of it he produced several rods that he assembled into a tall stand. He pulled out a small black box and fixed this to the top of the stand.

The strangers positioned themselves on either side of

Tambul's chair. The moustache threw himself on the ground in front, leaning on one elbow with one leg stretched out and the other bent. He looked like he was relaxing under a tree.

The moustache hurried back to the box and examined it. Then they rearranged themselves around the death chair again. This time, the moustache remained standing and the other two lay down in front of the chair.

The ancients exchanged baffled looks.

'What are they doing?' Dugas demanded. But of course, none of us could explain. Was it a ritual of some sort? What was in the box? Why were they striking different poses around Tambul's corpse?

We could do nothing but watch.

It felt like forever before Kinyo appeared on the path from the rice valley. He was running, hair slicked to his skull with sweat. Mister William followed close behind.

The Americans were astonished to see Mister William, though they seemed happy enough, reaching to clap him on the shoulder and shake his hand the way Kinyo had shaken ours the day before.

When they had first arrived, I had thought they all looked alike, apart from the moustache. But now I realized that they looked nothing alike: not their eyes, not their lips, not the widths of their shoulders.

Kinyo said the one with the moustache was called Corporal Quinlan. The other two were called Private Smith and Private Henry.

I wanted to say the names aloud – try the sound of them on my tongue. But now Salluyud was barking, 'Kinyo, ask them what they are doing with that box!'

Corporal Quinlan laughed as if Kinyo had made a joke.

'He says they are doing a kodak,' Kinyo translated.

'A kodak?' Blind Maklan muttered. 'What is a kodak?'

The American was holding up the box.

'That is a kodak,' Kinyo said. 'It is for making pictures. He says they are making pictures to show people in America.'

'But what is a picture?' Luki said.

Kinyo's lashes fluttered as he considered her question. He did not translate it for the Americans but answered it himself. 'That book Mister William tried to give the ancients. It had pictures in it. The kodak can see. It makes a likeness of what it sees so that anybody can see it.'

The kodak could *see*? A likeness that you could look at again? It didn't make sense.

Dugas made an exhaling noise, like a water buffalo surfacing in the mud. 'Look at that one – what is he doing?'

The one called Private Smith was leaning over Tambul, slipping the ceremonial necklace off the corpse's shoulders. He put it in his pocket. Then he grabbed the dead man's arm and began to twist the boar's tooth armband off.

'Stop him!' I cried. 'He's stealing Tambul's things!'

But nobody – not the warriors, not Father, not the ancients, not even Muddo who had wanted to fight them – made a move.

152

The American put the armband in his pocket and reached for the one on Tambul's other arm.

I didn't think. I just found myself there, slapping Private Smith's hand away from my friend's corpse and snatching the armband from his hand.

'THIEF!' I heard myself shout. 'Give that back!'

26

Private Smith's eyes held mine. They were not as brilliant a blue as Mister William's, but cloudier and stained with brown, like the Chico River after a big rain. The dog-hair bristles stood hard and proud on his top lip. There was a violent rushing in my ears, like water boiling on river rapids. I could vaguely hear the ancients scolding in the distance, and the deeper murmur of Mister William's voice. He sounded furious, as if he was chastising the other Americans. 'Samkad, get away!' I heard someone say. But I didn't – couldn't – move. An angry spirit had taken over my body. My arms and legs were not mine.

'Sam!' I heard Father call. 'Don't upset him, Sam.'

But the angry spirit inside me didn't care. '*THIEF!*' The word burst out of my throat again.

I heard Chuka growling. 'Luki, hold that dog!' Father called.

Suddenly the tip of a long metal cylinder was pressed against my forehead, hard and cold. Weh. So this was a gun? This was how the Americans brought death to their enemies? But my angry spirit felt no fear and my chin raised itself so that my forehead pressed harder against the gun.

Now Kinyo was squeaking behind me in a pleading voice. Hearing Kinyo beg in the thief's tongue made the spirit inside me burn hot. My mouth worked up a big gob of saliva. I spat on the American's foot, the spittle dribbling all over his hide-covered toes.

'*NO!*' I felt Father's hand on my shoulder now, yanking me back. His other hand snatched at Tambul's armband. 'Kinyo, tell the Americans he is just a child. Tell them they can have whatever they like!'

Now Mister William put his broad body between me and Private Smith, talking in a soothing, reasoning voice.

Private Smith sneered at Mister William, and replied in a jeering voice. He whipped the gun away from my forehead and waved it in the air. A hand appeared behind him and tried to snatch it away.

It was Corporal Quinlan. Private Smith held on but Corporal Quinlan twisted the the gun barrel up and up and up so that the other American ended up wriggling from its handle like a fish on a spear.

There was an explosion and the water buffalo skull atop the fern tree pillar shattered into a shower of bone.

A smell of burning filled the air. I found myself cowering,

both hands clamped over my deafened ears. It felt like the explosion had happened deep inside my head.

Private Smith allowed Corporal Quinlan to take the gun.

I swallowed and my hearing returned. I could hear Corporal Quinlan speaking in a soft explaining voice as Private Smith looked on with a surly expression on his face.

Kinyo translated. 'Corporal Quinlan says he is sorry.'

Sorry? The invader was apologising?

Kinyo frowned, concentrating, as Corporal Quinlan held his hand out and the thief handed back the necklace he had taken from Tambul. 'He says they have no quarrel with us. They want to become our friends. We can have the trinkets back.'

He held the necklace out at me.

I snatched it from him and quickly slipped under his outstretched arm to lay the necklace back on Tambul's headless shoulders.

Corporal Quinlan continued to speak and my brother translated breathlessly. 'He says, did you appreciate what the gun could do? Do you appreciate what a powerful gift this is?'

A *gift*?

The American held the stinking thing out to Father.

'They want us to have it,' Kinyo whispered. 'They want us to have the gun.'

27

The Americans nodded smugly to each other as they watched the men of Bontok surge forward. Even the ancients jostled to get near the gun. It shocked me to see the grins on their faces, the haste with which they snatched the gun from Father's hands, the way their eyes gleamed as they passed it around, the way they licked their lips as they stroked the long black tube, as if just touching it made their mouths run dry.

Father folded his arms across his chest, his lips compressed as the younger men badgered Kinyo to translate questions for the Americans.

'Ask him if it should be kept dry.'

'Ask him how it works.'

'Ask him for the missiles that go inside.'

The ancients were even worse. Their withered faces split into gummy smiles and they reached for the gun with their gnarled arms, like babies reaching for their mothers.

They all wanted it.

A gun, Samkad, a gun! I told myself. *Why aren't you excited? Did you not see what it could do? Don't you want it too? A better weapon than a spear, better than an axe.* But I felt no enthusiasm.

The gun was passed from hand to hand and the Americans smiled. They had demonstrated its power and now they were handing that power over to us. But what for? What did they want in exchange?

Corporal Quinlan whispered softly into Kinyo's ear.

'As you know, the Americans have been pursuing the low-lander army for many months now.'

As you know. Did *everyone* except me know about this war between the Americans and the lowlanders? I looked round. Nobody seemed even remotely surprised.

'Two days ago, not far from here, the lowlanders ambushed our soldiers.'

He named a mountain pass I had never heard of before . . . but Father and the ancients nodded.

Corporal Quinlan grinned so widely his roll of moustache stretched from ear to ear. He made a gesture like he was cutting his throat with a knife.

'Fifty-two,' Kinyo translated. 'The Americans killed fifty-two of the enemy. It was a slaughter.'

There was a sudden squawk from Private Smith and Private Henry. I stared at them, confused. They were laughing help-lessly, clutching their bellies, as if it was a hilarious joke.

158

Fifty-two souls taken from the lowlanders by the Americans. I felt a cold fist wrap itself around my heart. The Americans were comical to look at, with their huge feet and their large heads and hair the colour of dog sprouting all over their faces. But their guns made them the deadliest kind of enemy.

'There is a large contingent of American soldiers travelling through the pass soon,' Kinyo continued. 'The bodies need to be cleared. The American says they need our help.'

'Help? How can we help them?' Father said.

'They want us to bury the dead,' Kinyo said.

Bury the dead? I glanced at Tambul. We were supposed to be honouring Tambul as his soul eased into the world of the Uninvited. But the arrival of the Americans had stolen his time.

'Preposterous!' Salluyud shook the gun at the Americans. 'They give us *ONE* gun and they think we will clean up their mess!'

Kinyo looked nervously at Salluyud. 'Do . . . do I have to translate that?'

But, before anyone could say anything, Corporal Quinlan turned and barked something at the other two.

Kinyo's eyes widened. 'He says . . . he says—'

But Kinyo didn't have to translate. The American called Private Henry had already crossed the courtyard and handed *another* gun to Salluyud. The ancient stared at the two guns as if he'd suddenly sprouted a new pair of arms. The other men were already rushing towards him. They couldn't wait to touch it.

159

Father threw himself in front of them, his arms spread wide. 'Shame, shame, shame!' he cried. 'Have you been bewitched? Have you forgotten that we have to find the Mangili who murdered Tambul? We cannot leave the village unprotected!'

The ancients nodded. With a guilty look, Salluyud put the gun down on the ground. The other men frowned, chewing their lips. What the spirits of our ancestors must think to see our behaviour! How unforgivable to be ready to abandon one's people for the gifts of strangers!

Father told the Americans about Tambul's murder the night before and the importance of capturing his killers. As Kinyo translated, Corporal Quinlan exchanged looks with his men.

He began to speak rapidly.

Kinyo's eyes widened. 'He is saying that last night, while camping on the other side of the forest, they were attacked by two Mangili.'

'Two?' Father said. 'What did they do?'

'They shot them dead and buried them in a ditch.'

There was a silence.

Father's eyes were round. 'Is he sure they were Mangili?'

Corporal Quinlan nodded and Kinyo spoke his words.

'Yes. They know the Mangili well and these men definitely were Mangili. Corporal Quinlan says our enemy is dead and we have nothing to worry about now. The danger is over.'

Father shook his head. 'But how do we know that these were the same men who killed Tambul?'

The American looked at Tambul, sitting quietly in his funeral chair.

'The Mangili were carrying a basket,' Kinyo translated. 'Inside it was a man's head. When they buried the Mangili, they buried the head in its basket.'

Everyone was suddenly smiling. Surely this was excellent news. We were safe. And, even better than that, Tambul's head was there to be retrieved. But the cold fist was still hard around my heart. Why did I feel uneasy?

Salluyud turned to the other ancients. 'This is an even better gift than these guns,' he said. 'Tambul's spirit will be appeased to know that we can retrieve his head and he can be buried with dignity. His ghost will not haunt us.'

'Kinyo.' Father looked grim. 'Ask them if they can show us where they buried the Mangili so that we can reclaim Tambul's head. Tell them it is important we return it to his body before he is buried.'

Kinyo translated in a quavering voice.

Corporal Quinlan nodded vigorously.

'The American says this is no problem – they are pleased to kill our enemy for us,' Kinyo said. 'They will take us to where they buried them so that we can recover the head.'

'Lumawig be praised!' the ancients began to cry, clasping their hands and closing their eyes with joy.

The American grinned and whispered something to Kinyo.

Kinyo licked his lips. 'They will do all this and we can keep the guns. But we must agree to bury their dead.'

161

Everyone was exclaiming now and the guns were lifted up and passed from hand to hand.

I peered up at Corporal Quinlan, who was watching with arms folded across his chest. He was smiling. But the muddy eyes under the thick eyebrows flitted about like a fish in search of feed.

28

It was agreed.

Twenty men, plus Kinyo as their interpreter, would accompany the Americans to the mountain pass to bury the dead. On the way, the Americans were going to show them where the Mangili were buried, so that they could retrieve Tambul's head and bury his corpse as a whole man.

The ancients had dispatched a messenger to the caves to tell everyone that all was safe, there was no longer any enemy to fear and everyone could return to the village. They ordered Kinyo to invite the Americans to some rice and pork for breakfast.

Kinyo hurried to speak to the Americans, but Private Smith and Private Henry were mounting their horses and preparing to ride back down to the mossy forest. Corporal Quinlan ignored Kinyo and fetched the kodak.

'They said they had to do a survey of the area,' Kinyo told the ancients. 'To make sure all is secure.'

'What about him?' Dugas said, tilting his head towards Corporal Quinlan, sauntering through the village.

'He is their commander and he can do what he likes,' Kinyo shrugged.

Luki, Kinyo and I sat on our heels, watching as the American took the kodak out of his bag and began to set up its stand. I realized he wanted to make more pictures. Of our huts. Of the women returning to their fires. Of the children playing on the trails. Of the chickens scratching in the dirt.

How faithfully did his kodak duplicate what it saw? Could it see what lay within as well? Did its pictures capture our souls too? And if it did, what was going to happen when he took our souls away to America?

I felt a tap on my shoulder. It was Father, balancing bowls of rice and salted pork on one arm. 'The ancients say you must eat now so that we can leave as soon as possible,' he said gruffly. 'The sooner we go, the sooner we can return to keep Tambul's vigil.'

I looked across at Tambul's corpse, sitting stiffly in his chair. Several of his friends were gathered around the funeral chair, chatting with the headless body to show his spirit their respect. My dead friend's broad shoulders were now sloping over the rope that bound his chest to the chair. One knee had collapsed inward.

I remembered my dream, staring into the shadow mouth

howling in the head of flames. If Tambul was buried with his head, the spirits of our ancestors would look more kindly upon him and might invite him into their invisible world. Perhaps he could be spared the horror of being one of the Uninvited.

Father tossed a strip of pork up in the air and Chuka caught it in mid-air, swallowing without even bothering to chew. She gave him an ingratiating smile, her swollen eye making her look lopsided.

'Enough, Chuka!' I commanded, nervous that she might do something to displease him.

Father smiled. 'It's all right. I understand. This dog's soul has become attached to you, Samkad.' He sighed. 'She reminds me of a dog I used to keep when I was a boy. I know what it's like to have a dog love me. I named him Asin.'

Father had a *dog*?

How could he have warned me away from dogs when he himself had kept one? He even named it! I sneaked a glance at Luki. She was gaping so wide I could see a small ball of rice making its way down the back of her throat.

'It cannot be helped. Sometimes a beast just chooses you,' Father continued. 'Asin chose me.' Father smoothed his hand over Chuka's ears and she quickly flipped over on her back, inviting Father to rub her tummy.

'What happened to your dog?' Kinyo asked, his voice muffled under a mouthful of rice.

A shadow crossed Father's face. 'He died,' he said softly. Then he shook his head. 'No. He didn't just die. He was chosen.'

'Chosen?' Luki said.

Father nodded. 'At the time, we were at war with the village of Talubin. The Talubin despised us and we despised them and they hunted us and we hunted them and on and on our struggle went. The Talubin wore us out, hunting us like animals. So many children became orphans. We needed to overwhelm the Talubin, attack them once and for all so that they would leave us alone, end the war. But our men had become weakened by fear. And the spirits of our ancestors forgot about us, we were getting no help from them. Or maybe they were cowed by the fierceness of our enemy.'

Father's hand paused on Chuka's head. 'We needed new courage. So the ancients chose Asin. They sent his soul into the world of the dead, so that our ancestors might pay us heed and his fierce spirit would give us courage.'

I stared at Chuka. At first I had thought her a silly dog, always wanting love and attention. But she was not silly at all. These past few days she had proven herself ferocious and loyal.

'He died quickly – he was so eager to do his work,' Father said softly. 'Even as his blood filled the ancients' bowl, his soul was already roaring through the invisible world. And it worked. Our village defeated the Talubin so comprehensively that they agreed to a truce, which holds to this day.'

'It looks to me that the more Chuka serves you, Samkad, the fiercer she becomes.' Father was rubbing Chuka's belly now, his face averted. The black dog wriggled with pleasure. 'Good dog.'

At that moment Chuka rolled back onto her front, her one good eye narrowed. Her lips curled to reveal vicious teeth and she growled.

'What is it, dog?' I said softly.

But now she was on her feet and rushing headlong down the path.

'Samkad, hold that dog or the Americans might do something to her,' Father said through gritted teeth. But I was already rushing after her, my rice bowl tumbling to the ground.

'Chuka!' I gritted my teeth. The dog was darting down the path, heading directly for Private Smith and Private Henry, who were leading their horses towards us.

The horses reared and swerved as Chuka flew at them. The Americans yelled at her, whipping their hats off to swat her away.

But Chuka was not aiming for them.

She scampered just beyond reach of their hooves before she froze, every muscle rigid, teeth bared. A low, angry growl rolled from deep in her throat. And her eyes glared as if she had come face to face with her most hated enemy.

Behind the horses, someone returned the dog's glare. Someone with wrists bound, tethered to one of the horses by a long rope.

I recognized him immediately.

It was the Mangili who had attacked me in the rice valley.

29

Of course I recognized him. I had wiped the mud off his face with my own hands. There was no mistaking those eyes, the thick brows, the short hair.

Private Henry stomped across to the dog and, hooking his great foot under her belly, flicked her away as if she was a bothersome piece of rubbish.

Chuka yelped as she tumbled to the side of the path, but wasted no time flipping back onto her feet to snap at the American.

'No!' I threw myself over Chuka in case the American drew his gun. 'Kinyo, tell him the dog means no harm!'

While Kinyo placated Private Henry, I began to drag Chuka back up the hill. She resisted, planting her paws in the dirt, by turns whining and growling, unwilling to leave her enemy, who smirked to see me struggle. He recognized me, I was sure of it. Father was watching us from the top of the hill.

'Father! Come, quickly! It is him! Look!'

'It is who, Samkad?'

I waved one hand at the Americans' prisoner while holding Chuka down with the other. 'It's the Mangili who attacked me in the rice valley!'

Father had an odd expression on his face. Slowly, he approached the horse. Private Smith and Private Henry eyed him with suspicion as he did so.

'Son,' Father said softly. 'This man is not a Mangili.'

'But he is! I wrestled with him in Second Best Valley.'

Kinyo, tailing Father, made a funny face. 'Your father is right. This man can't be a Mangili. He's a lowlander.' He shouted something at the Americans, listening carefully as they replied.

'They are saying that they caught him hiding up a tree in the forest,' Kinyo said.

Father put his arm around my shoulders. 'He is a soldier, son. A soldier of the lowlander army.'

'But I thought . . .'

'See how he's dressed?' Father said patiently. 'Didn't I tell you the Mangili wear breechcloths like we do? This is how a lowlander soldier is dressed.'

I looked at the American's prisoner. His torso was bare, but I saw now that what Father said was true: his legs and waist were clad in the same sort of cloth wrapping worn by Kinyo and the Americans.

The prisoner grimaced at me. He spat in the dirt and Chuka would have flown at him had I not dragged her away.

It took Father, Kinyo and Luki to help me pull the dog back

169

to our hut. I pushed her in and shut the door. We all sighed with relief.

Father put one hand on my shoulder, the other on Kinyo's.

'These are extraordinary times. I hope you boys understand that,' he said.

I nodded, even though I was confused. I had blamed myself when Tambul died. I thought he had died because I had not warned the ancients about the Mangili in the valley. But now it turned out my opponent had not been a Mangili at all.

'My sons, you both have important roles to fulfil when it becomes time to keep our promise to the Americans. Kinyo, we will need you to speak to the Americans. And you, Sam, will come with us to where they buried the Mangili. We will exhume Tambul's head and you will carry it back to the village while we travel on to the burial site. We will honour Tambul by reuniting his body with his head.'

Luki was watching us with wide eyes. She stepped forward. 'Please, let me come too. I can help Sam bring Tambul's head back.'

Father smiled at Luki. 'It is very kind of you to offer, but this is a job for a man and not a girl. Your duty is to return to your mother, Chochon . . . she will be here soon from the caves and there will be many chores she will need you to do.'

Luki's mango face twisted.

Father turned away from her. 'Sam, Kinyo, I have not forgotten that you should have had the Cut this morning,' he said.

In fact, I *had* forgotten. Kinyo made a choking noise. He

had forgotten too. I was surprised to find myself indifferent. The Cut didn't seem to matter much right now.

Father looked at me, his eyes serious. 'I want you to know that you made me proud when you stood up to that American, when nobody else was willing to do it. To me, you have proven beyond doubt that you are a man. Cut or no cut.' He smiled. 'I promise, once the Americans are gone, we will follow the proper ceremonies.'

I felt a surge of warmth in my belly. Father had never spoken to me that way before. 'Kinyo.' Father turned to my brother. 'I am sorry that your homecoming has been so . . . difficult. I had wanted to celebrate your return. I promise, once this business is over, that you will get the welcome you deserve. I want you to know I am proud of you and your gift with different tongues.'

'Thank you . . . Father,' Kinyo whispered, tracing the dirt with his toe.

Father smiled at Luki. 'Sam became a man yesterday. He stood up for Tambul against the Americans when no one had the courage to do it.'

Luki made a huffing noise. 'So . . .' she was pouting. 'If it had been *me* who argued with the American . . . would you call *me* a man today?'

Father laughed. 'Luki! You are incorrigible!' He winked at her as he began to walk away. 'Come on, Kinyo, son. The ancients need you to talk to the Americans now.'

Luki's eyes fixed on me as Father and Kinyo left. Weh, her eyes were wet and her mouth was turned down so hard that it was a wonder her jaw had not dropped off her face.

'What's the matter with you?' I mumbled.

She scowled. 'Huh, do you know what that was all about, Samkad? Your father was just soothing your feelings because it's going to be weeks before anybody will have time to give you the Cut.'

'It doesn't matter when they give me the Cut, does it?' I growled. 'Father said so himself!'

I couldn't believe it. All the sweet exhilaration I had felt at Father's words dissipated. Why did she act like this every time we talked about my manhood? What sort of friend would trample on your ambitions?

'The problem with you is that you're jealous that I'm going to become a man!' I snapped.

'Jealous? Why should I be jealous?'

'You hate that I'm finally going to become a man.'

'No, I don't.' Her mouth twisted. 'I really don't.'

'Look at you. Since we were little you have wanted to dress like a boy. Play like a boy. Fight like a boy. You wish you were me, don't you?'

Luki's fists were bunched up. I felt my own fingers curl into themselves. My gut was boiling.

'Hah. You think a man is just someone with a cut foreskin who's allowed to carry a spear and a shield,' Luki cried.

I allowed my fist to fly. Put all my weight into it. It caught the side of her head. Whipped her face sideways. Chuka yelped as if it was her that I had struck.

I glanced round me. Nobody had seen me hit Luki. At my feet, Chuka whimpered.

I waited for Luki's own fist to fly. I decided that I would allow her to hit me back and then that was it. We were done. We could put an end to this strange friendship that never should have been. A girl playing like a boy? It had always been ridiculous and everyone knew it.

'Come on,' I snarled. 'You want to be a man too? Then hit me back. Hit me like a man.'

Her eyes were dark and moist.

'A man never cries!' I hissed. 'You're a fraud and you know it, Luki! You will never become a man and that is why you hate the idea of me becoming one.'

The tears came faster, streaming down her cheeks in shining trails. But Luki didn't wipe them away.

'You're right,' she said. 'I hate the idea of you becoming a man. I hate it because when you become a man you are going to have to stop being my friend.'

She turned round.

'Where are you going?' I called.

She glanced briefly over her shoulder. 'I'm going to see if my mother has any chores for me in the House for Women.'

There was a soft whimper.

'What do you want, Chuka?' I mumbled.

But the dog was already away, trotting at Luki's heels.

30

Soon Father had gathered together the twenty men the Americans needed for their task. They sat on their heels, around Tambul's death chair, digging tools cradled in their arms, axes at their waists, and baskets of provisions on their backs, waiting for the signal to move on. Mister William stood by the fern tree pillar, now minus its water buffalo skull. I didn't know what else to do, so I squatted down to join them.

But now Corporal Quinlan was setting up the kodak in front of the ancients. Kinyo translated as the American cajoled the old men to stand in a row.

'He says please stay very still,' Kinyo told them. 'And please try not to cover the tattoos on your chest.'

After a minute Corporal Quinlan flashed his teeth at the ancients and bowed. 'He wants to show you something,' Kinyo said.

The American held up a small box from which he extracted a stick. It was a thin splinter the length of a finger, with a swollen red tip. He beamed at us, as if he expected us all to jump up and down with excitement. Holding the stick high, he snatched up one of the wooden bowls lying by the fire. Over it he waved the stick in a spiral, the way Salluyud would whirl the shoulder bone of a water buffalo over the fire to invoke our ancestors. Then, slowly, slowly, he scraped the stick's red tip across the bowl's wooden lip. There was a crackle and then, with a loud hiss, it burst into flame.

We were all on our feet. Looking around me, I could see my own utter amazement in the faces of the others: open mouths and wide eyes that were both bewildered and impressed.

'This is how Americans make fire,' Kinyo translated.

Afterwards, Corporal Quinlan distributed one fire stick to each of us. As I pushed forward to receive my stick, I glanced at the other Americans. Mister William's lipless mouth was pursed, as if he'd eaten a sour tamarind. And the noses of Private Smith and Private Henry were curled in sneers. Perhaps they had wanted the fire sticks for themselves.

I had never seen the ancients smile such huge gap-toothed smiles as they accepted their sticks and shook Corporal Quinlan's hand, in the way that Kinyo had demonstrated when he first arrived. Before I tucked it into my belt, I stared at mine for a long time, turning it over and sniffing it. So small and yet so powerful not to need tinder or pitch or the spark of a stone to create a flame.

Later, the Americans ordered the digging party into a column, with Corporal Quinlan in front, Private Smith and Private Henry in the back, and everyone else in between. Quinlan positioned Kinyo and me just behind his horse, with the prisoner, who was still roped to his horse. Father lingered on the side, discussing something with the ancients. I was not really listening until his voice rose. 'But there is still danger!'

'Danger!' Salluyud was replying, his old face puckered with annoyance. 'Those two Mangili are dead. Their people will still be waiting for their return. Now is the safest time to leave the village. And the more men you take, the more quickly the job will be done.'

Maklan had a smug grin on his face. 'When you dig up those dead Mangili, make sure you tell their corpses, "Next time, pick another village to attack."'

'Don't forget,' Pito added, 'we have guns now.'

Only then did I notice that two men were standing by the path cradling the American guns in their arms. One was Lamang, a potter with a belly that poured over his breech-cloth. The other was Dipa, whose wife had only recently had a baby.

Father looked slantways at the two and shook his head. 'You need more than those two to guard the forest.'

'Each gun is equal to ten men,' Dugas declared.

Lamang, catching Father's eye, made explosive noises with his mouth.

Father looked away. Then he sighed and rose, waving at Kinyo and me, as he joined the other men in the middle of the column. But he was still worried. I could tell by the creases cutting deep on either side of his jaw.

Corporal Quinlan was rummaging in his pack. He grabbed something and hurried round his horse to the prisoner before kneeling on one knee.

Curious, I leaned forward to see what he could be doing as he bent over the lowlander's feet.

He was fastening iron bands to the young man's ankles. The bands were connected by a short, heavy chain. Why would he shackle the lowlander's ankles now? Weren't we just about to set off?

Realizing that I was watching, the American smiled warmly as he got back up on his feet. He ruffled Kinyo's hair, handing him something out of his pocket. Kinyo exclaimed over it with delight, beaming as Corporal Quinlan turned to mount his horse. Kinyo held it up to me. 'He said we should share this.'

'What is it?'

'Sweets. You know, like Mister William's gumdrop. Here, try it.'

I shook my head, remembering the shock of the gumdrop on my tongue.

Kinyo put it in his mouth and smiled blissfully. 'It's really good!' he said. 'Better than gumdrops – but don't tell Mister William!'

Corporal Quinlan climbed up on his horse and twisted around holding his hand high. The two Americans in the back responded with a shout and Kinyo translated, his voice shrill above the murmurs of the men. 'Time to go!'

He waved at Mister William, who waved back, lipless mouth twitching in a small smile. The way he looked at the other Americans was odd; it was definitely not the gaze of a friend.

Chuka was nowhere to be seen. Resentment prickled in my chest. She was with Luki, no doubt. It was just as well. The Americans did not want her around and she would have been impossible with the prisoner close by.

Just as we began to move down the mountain, Corporal Quinlan's horse suddenly bolted forward.

It took the lowlander unawares. He fell on his knees and was dragged a short way. Corporal Quinlan glanced over his shoulder as Kinyo and I grabbed the prisoner by the elbows and helped him back on his feet. He had to adopt an odd shuffling movement to avoid tripping on his shackles.

Down the mountain we went, the hot sun warming our heads and prompting a wave of storytelling from the throats of the men around us, vivid tellings of long-ago clashes with the Mangili, the number of heads lost and reaped, the valour of the men who had fought.

But then we entered the forest and almost immediately the happy chatter was sucked away, absorbed by the moss that wadded every crevice and dressed every branch and boulder.

In that strange, padded atmosphere the men ceased their chatter, until the only sounds to be heard were the *hnhh hnhh* of their breathing, the snort and clop of the horses, the heavy clink of the lowlander's shackles, and, somewhere up ahead, the murmur of the Tree of Bones.

31

At first I thought Corporal Quinlan just wanted to make sure that the prisoner was keeping up. The American kept glancing over his shoulder at the lowlander, whose bare shoulders were bright with sweat as he lurched along.

But then I saw the American grin. Yet again he jabbed his heels into his horse. Yet again it jerked forward. Yet again the lowlander was yanked off his feet.

Corporal Quinlan didn't make any attempt to slow the horse down once the lowlander was prone in the dirt behind him. He just kept urging it on, even as Kinyo and I chased behind, trying to help the lowlander back on his feet. By the time we'd managed it, the prisoner was scratched and bleeding and covered with moss and tiny specks of grit.

He'd only been up for a few heartbeats when Corporal Quinlan did it again. His horse burst into a trot. And down went the lowlander.

And over and over again.

It was as if the American was two people. The one who made the ancients smile and shook our hands and offered us sweets. And this one. Who enjoyed watching his prisoner stumble and fall.

You cannot help someone as many times as we got the low-lander to his feet and still not know his name. Lowlander was one of the languages that Kinyo carried in his throat and soon he was collecting little mouthfuls of information about the prisoner.

'He says his name is Juan,' Kinyo whispered.

And then: 'He says he ran away during a battle.'

And then: 'He wants to go home. But his family is dead.'

'You sound like you pity him,' I said.

Kinyo shrugged. 'Don't you?'

'I thought you liked the Americans.'

'I like Mister William.' Kinyo scowled. 'Mister William is different. He is not an invader.'

I mused on this as we walked deeper into the mossy forest. Was it possible to be friends with one American and the enemy of another? Could I, a Bontok, ever be friends with a Mangili?

What was important, I decided, was to retrieve Tambul's head. We only had to get along with the Americans until we had fulfilled our part of the bargain. And then they could go away and leave us alone forever.

The murmuring had become louder. The path was

meandering towards the clearing where the Tree of Bones waited. I wondered what the spirits would say as we filed past.

But Corporal Quinlan turned his horse's head and led us down another path.

'We've taken a wrong turn!' Father called from behind.

Kinyo scrambled alongside the American, translating. But Corporal Quinlan didn't even glance down.

Father pushed past the other men and joined us in front. 'Kinyo, can he not hear you? Tell him this way does not go to the place where they said they buried the Mangili. We must change direction.'

Kinyo hurried on, squeaking at the American until, at last, Corporal Quinlan raised his hand, calling everyone to a stop. He turned his horse and leaned down towards Kinyo, plucking the ends of his moustache as Kinyo translated Father's message.

But before Kinyo had ceased talking, Corporal Quinlan whipped his horse away, the lowlander floundering behind him, and trotted past Father, the huge hooves so close that Father had to jump to the side to avoid getting trampled. The American shouted something curtly over his shoulder.

'What did he say?' Father asked. 'Why is he continuing on?'

'He says no,' Kinyo said. 'He wants us to reach the pass by morning. There is no time to dig up the Mangili now. He says it can wait. We must do the burying first.'

'But he promised!' Father's face darkened with anger. 'That is why Samkad is with us, to take Tambul's head back to the village.' He raced after the American, leaping to grab the halter of Corporal Quinlan's horse.

I watched anxiously as they glared at each other. Was Father going to draw his axe? Was Corporal Quinlan going to pull out his gun?

From the back of the column there was a sharp scream. And then . . . barking.

Corporal Quinlan pushed Father away and turned his horse.

The men behind us were making a raucous noise now. The sound was not angry or fearful. Were they *laughing*?

And then I recognized the shrill, complaining voice that rose over all the clamour. Luki.

'Let go of me, American! Let go!' Luki screeched.

Private Henry was trotting towards us with Luki flopped over the neck of his horse. Chuka yapped and snapped at his heels. The horse stopped in front of Corporal Quinlan and Private Henry tossed Luki down onto the ground.

Chuka jumped onto Luki as she struggled to her feet, whimpering and licking. She stared up at Corporal Quinlan, cheeks tear-smeared, but eyes sparking with defiance. She was dressed in her shabby old breechcloth again.

'The American is asking if you know this boy,' Kinyo said, staring with fascination at Luki's costume.

'She is *not* a boy,' Father said through gritted teeth. 'What are you doing here, Luki?' He grabbed her hand as if he would lead her straight back to the village right there and then, but Luki pulled away.

'I told you. I wanted to come too.'

'She was meant to stay with her mother,' Father told the American. 'I am sorry, she's always been headstrong—'

But now Corporal Quinlan was roaring something in his deep voice.

'What?' Father snapped. 'What's he saying now?'

'Time,' Kinyo said. 'He is saying this is a waste of his time.'

The American pulled the gun from his belt and pointed it at Luki.

The joking of the men behind us dwindled to silence.

'What does he think he's doing with that gun? What is he saying now?' Luki demanded, her chest thrust out.

Kinyo darted at Luki, and shoved her towards the forest.

'He said: RUN, Luki!'

Luki ran.

The American fired his gun.

The first explosion, and Chuka bolted after Luki.

The second explosion, they were almost at the trees.

The third explosion, and clumps of leaves fell as Luki was swallowed by the forest.

Corporal Quinlan shrugged his shoulders, tucked the gun away and kicked his horse back into motion, his face bored.

I bolted after Luki, but Father's hands snatched me back. 'No, Sam.'

Corporal Quinlan had already disappeared round a bend with the lowlander and Kinyo close behind. The other two Americans were shouting and waving their hats, urging the other men along like you would herd a water buffalo to the paddy fieds. Father's hands turned me towards them. 'Come, Sam. She will be fine.'

I resisted. 'What if Luki is hurt?'

'She isn't. I saw her get safely away.'

'But I should make sure she's all right.'

Father guided me firmly back to the group. 'She's fine. Chuka has gone after her and will be her protector. And anyway, there is no danger in the forest now that the Mangili who attacked Tambul are dead,' he said. 'Son, stay with me and your brother. We need you.'

We need you. I obeyed Father, hurrying to the front of the column to take my place behind Corporal Quinlan's horse. I stared at the American's tall back and the swaying haunches of his horse . . . and Juan, tripping and struggling at the end of his rope.

Father was wrong. There was danger. And it was not just in the forest behind us.

32

Climbing uphill, the giant horses towered above us, their monster heads like nodding cliffs, hooves kicking dung and dust into our faces, their hot, beasty odour infusing the air. The trail plunged downwards and we found ourselves gazing down upon their great, swaggering, sweat-shiny rumps.

We crossed from one mountain to the next along narrow traverses so precarious that the Americans had no choice but to dismount and lead their horses. The great beasts made their way across, the whites of their eyes showing, shying nervously at the gorges on either side.

When the ground became broader and flatter, the Americans re-mounted and Corporal Quinlan kicked his horse into a quick trot, watching with a small smile as Juan stumbled and fell. As the horse dragged him along, the lowlander could only tuck his face into his shoulder and wait until

Kinyo and I could put him back on his feet. He was thoroughly exhausted now, and his wounds were gaping and bloody from the repeated gouging of stones.

Kinyo and I had picked him up so often that the whole process had become mundane. It had somehow become normal for the American to cause the lowlander to fall. And still even more normal for us to pick him up. We had done it so many times it was no longer something to be upset about.

So the next time Juan fell I was startled to find Father running alongside us, his axe raised. He barged us aside. Down the axe went with a loud clink. The chain hobbling Juan's ankles flew apart.

'Hup, hup!' Corporal Quinlan clicked his tongue and kicked the horse into another trot. Father slipped an arm around Juan's waist, lifting him bodily onto his feet. I saw the American glance over his shoulder. His blue eyes became small and hard as they flitted from Father to Juan, now running easily behind the horse, the cut lengths of chain from each ankle clinking against the ground.

For a moment, I was afraid he would explode his gun at Father.

But he just returned his attention to the trail and urged his horse on.

We arrived at a river, fed by springs from higher up in the mountain. The water was an intense blue and we could see every stone that paved the bed below. It was perhaps waist-high to a man. But it was broad and the water rushed swift and strong, spitting ruffs of foam.

The horses reared and bit and complained, pawing the river bank, flaring their nostrils. Their animal smell intensified with their fear.

They would not cross.

The Americans dismounted and, through Kinyo, commanded the men to lead the horses across the river.

When Father joined the men surrounding the beasts, Corporal Quinlan wagged a finger at him, smiling.

'He says not you,' Kinyo said. 'He's got another job for you.'

The men plunged into the river, clucking and whistling and clutching the horses' manes. The great beasts bared their huge teeth and shook their heads, dragging Juan behind them. We watched on the shore, Father, Kinyo and me, standing slightly away from the Americans.

It took an age. The animals shied in the crashing water, their hooves beating down on the boiling swirl. Juan gurgled in the water, half swimming, half drowning.

At last the men and horses emerged on the other side. The horses wandered off calmly to crop the grass in the shade, Juan still stumbling behind them. The lowlander threw himself on the ground next to the beasts, eyes closed, his chest rising and falling.

The men sat on the grassy banks, eyeing us on the other side. What next?

Corporal Quinlan whispered instructions into Kinyo's ear. My brother's cheeks suddenly tinged with red.

'What's wrong? What did he say?' Father said.

Kinyo swallowed. 'He said . . . squat.'

'Squat?' I said. 'Are you sure? What for?'

'He says they-they-they don't want to get th-th-their clothes wet,' Kinyo began to stutter. 'He says y-y-you must carry them over.' Kinyo looked at Father with fearful eyes. 'I'm sorry. I'm sorry.'

Father was silent. Corporal Quinlan folded his arms across his chest and smirked.

Father nodded. He handed his digging stick to me, then unstrapped the basket of food from his back and gave it to Kinyo to carry.

He lowered himself onto his heels.

Across the river, the men sat up.

Corporal Quinlan swung one leg over Father's shoulder. And then his other leg. Father rose easily even though the man on his shoulders was more than a head taller than him. The American grinned, swaying ever so slightly, his hands on his hips, surveying the world, as Father stepped into the water, planting every foot with care.

I avoided Father's eyes. It would shame him to see me looking. But I needn't have bothered. Father's eyes were resolutely fixed on the opposite shore.

Five times Father had to cross the river, carrying each American across then returning to fetch another.

I tried not to watch, concentrating on making my own way across with Kinyo, who was holding our provisions basket above his head while I carried Father's digging stick high above the water. When we got to the other side, the men had turned their backs to the river so as not to watch Father's humiliation.

When all the Americans were across, they stretched their arms and twisted this way and that to soften their bodies before climbing back up onto their horses. They were smiling. Crossing the river had put them in a good mood.

Corporal Quinlan led his horse to the front of the column. He was just about to mount when somehow his eyes settled on Kinyo and me. He smiled, reaching into his pocket.

I did not expect it. He held something out to me and I was so surprised I reached up and took it. It was square and small and wrapped in something that was not fabric. Kinyo accepted his with a bright smile.

'The Americans call it "fudge",' Kinyo said, 'Just take the wrapper off like this.' He grabbed mine and quickly stripped away the thing that was not cloth to reveal a brown coloured square. He handed it back to me then unwrapped his and popped it straight into his mouth. 'It's delicious!'

I suddenly realized that the American had not mounted the horse. He stood there, smiling, as if he was waiting for something. As if the sticky brown square in the palm of my hand was something I had always wanted. As if I should show him gratitude after the way he had treated Father and Luki.

I felt something sharp stabbing in my gut. It was the angry spirit.

The angry spirit closed my fist over the sweet and made me draw back my arm. Then it made me throw the fudge, as hard as I could, into the American's face.

33

It struck him hard enough to make a thin little noise as it bounced off his nose. The smile slowly dripped from the American's face and a tiny red fire flickered in his eyes.

What had I done? The angry spirit was gone instantly, replaced by a horrible sense of dismay. Kinyo was staring at me, his mouth open so that I could see a tiny, uneaten piece of fudge still on his tongue.

Suddenly Father was there. He squeezed into the space between me and Corporal Quinlan, shouldering me away as he crouched, his head bowed, hands uplifted in supplication. He was mumbling in a voice I had not heard him use before. It was a begging voice, full of fear and weakness and submission.

'Please, please, my son is only a child. Translate, Kinyo! Please, my son does not know what he's doing – please forgive him. Kinyo! Are you translating? It was just a naughty impulse –

I will punish him for it, I promise. Please forgive, forgive, forgive.'

And I watched my father, our village's greatest warrior, bend down and touch his forehead on the American's foot.

The American said nothing. He carefully removed his foot from under Father's forehead and, turning, mounted his horse. Father remained where he was, as if he felt that the shame he had endured was still not enough.

I glanced over my shoulder and saw the horrified looks on the faces of the men behind us.

Corporal Quinlan kicked his horse and the column began to move off.

Only then did Father get back onto his feet.

The Americans chose a treeless place to stop for the night, where the dirt was packed and hard, as if it had not rained forever. The moon had long risen by that time, and the black of the sky was hung with thousands of stars, tiny and glinting like fireflies in a tree.

Corporal Quinlan summoned Kinyo to his side and, gathering us all together, he told us we would be arriving at our destination before the end of tomorrow morning. He said we would have to dig a trench and then explained at length how he wanted it done, such-and-such a width and such-and-such a depth and how the bodies of the dead would be neatly stacked and how, afterwards, we could fill the trench with soil and stone. Afterwards, he opened his box of fire sticks and began handing them out again, one to each man. Father joined the queue of men and smiled and thanked the American with an ingratiating little bob of his chin. It made me feel sick to see it and I pretended to be busy searching for something in our provisions to avoid being invited to the queue – I had no desire to look into the American's face. When Kinyo joined me later, he was holding up his own fire stick and chewing on another piece of fudge.

Fires were built – we had ours on one end of the clearing while the Americans built theirs on the opposite side. Funnily enough, nobody attempted to use a fire stick to light the fire. Perhaps everyone was saving its magic to show off at home. Then the men settled for the night, squatting in the dirt to eat, or unrolling their blankets and curling up to sleep.

I was hungry after our long day of walking, but I could barely eat the rice, parcelled in banana leaves, that Father offered from his basket

Father sent Kinyo to ask the Americans if he should organize a rota to keep watch through the night. But this only made the Americans argue amongst themselves, at the end of which Corporal Quinlan told Kinyo that they would keep watch; they didn't need any help from our men. Later, Kinyo said Corporal Quinlan had warned the other two that he didn't trust us not to run away.

I looked at Father to see what he thought about it. But there was a great shadow lying on his face.

Running away sounded like a good idea, I thought, wearily. Leave the Americans to bury the men they murdered.

*

Soon everyone was spread across the clearing like so many stones. Father, Kinyo and I lay together in a far corner. I could feel every bone of Father's spine against my back and Kinyo's elbow lay just short of my nose. I stared across the huddled bodies at the horses silhouetted against the fire. Somewhere in the darkness, Juan was still tied to the horse.

The others were soon asleep, their snores combining with the steady trill of night crickets. The star-spattered sky pressed down on our heads and I could feel the ache of the day in my limbs, but sleep would not come.

To think I was only supposed to retrieve Tambul's head. But now here I was.

And then, perhaps, I slept because when I opened my eyes Kinyo's knees were needling into the small of my back. I reached out to touch Father. He wasn't there.

'Please.'

It was a whisper somewhere in the blackness.

Hairs rose on my arms as I peered into the night. There was someone standing in the middle of that field of bodies, head thrown back as if he was searching for something in the night sky. He held his arms out like a toddler begging to be lifted up.

'Please.' The word caught in a sob, deep in his throat.

It was Father's voice.

Slowly, I got to my feet and crept towards him, stepping over slumbering bodies.

There was enough moonlight to see that his eyes were open.

But they were blank as they stared skyward. And the muscles on his face were slack. His breathing was deep. He was dreaming.

'Father?' I whispered.

'No,' he murmured. 'Not you!'

I looked over my shoulder fearfully, expecting to see the looming outline of Corporal Quinlan, waving his gun. But there was only the yellow moon and the glinting sky.

I took Father's hand. He did not resist as I led him back to our sleeping place. He walked blindly, stepping on someone's hand by mistake, kicking an outstretched leg. The sleeping men stirred and murmured at the disturbance but soon returned to their dreams.

I pulled Father down to the ground. He sighed as I pushed his head down. I lay myself next to him and stroked his arm, listening to his breathing deepen.

The ancients say one who walks in his dreams is walking in the realm of the spirits.

Not you, Father had said.

Not who?

When the Americans shouted us awake, the night crickets were still chirping and there was a veil of grey over everything.

Father was already sitting on his heels, eating a sweet potato from our provisions. His face was haggard, the lines on either side of his mouth deeply etched, and his eyes bloodshot.

'I have boiled eggs here, for you and your brother,' he said, holding out a banana-leaf parcel.

'I'm starving!' Kinyo cried, grabbing it eagerly.

'Father, are you all right?' I asked tentatively.

He looked at me, expressionless. 'Why do you ask?'

'Last night, something woke me up . . . and you were dream-walking.'

I told him what happened, trying to make his eyes meet mine.

But Father turned his eyes away and fixed his gaze on the ground.

'Do you remember what it was you were dreaming about?' I said. 'Why were you dream-walking?'

But now Father was on his feet. 'Eat up, boys,' he said. 'We will be off soon.' He set off to busy himself around the camp, rousing the men who had not yet awoken.

When we continued with the journey, he looked distracted, his eyes twitching everywhere, alighting on the stones under our feet and up the trees that walled either side of the trail, as if he was looking for something. Every unexpected noise made him startle.

Anger boiled in my breast. It was Corporal Quinlan's fault. He had humiliated Father, making him carry them across the river when they were perfectly capable of crossing by themselves. In my mind I marched up to Corporal Quinlan and tapped him on the shoulder. *Go away and take your guns with you!* I yelled. *Leave us alone!*

But of course I did nothing of the sort.

By the time the sun had turned into a tiny white disc in

the sky we had crossed yet another ridge to another mountain. This mountain was different from the others we'd passed through. There were no more green woods now. No more tiny threading streams, no more trees, no more wet, dripping moss.

It was hot, and the dry air sat in our throats like sand. We made a descent down a long trail made of narrow, sloping shelves of stone. The gravel under our feet moved and rolled like something alive, making the horses nervous. They whinnied and trembled, their hooves slipping and clattering. The Americans were forced to dismount and lead their horses.

A fat blowfly hummed near my sweaty head, its sticky wings brushing against my ear. Every time I tried to slap it, it darted out of reach. It didn't take us long to realize that the blowflies were everywhere, circling the rumps of the horses, evading the slap and swish of their tails, humming in and out of the column of men, hovering close over our heads, getting into our eyes and mouths. There were so many it seemed as if the air had turned grey.

And then I noticed the stench.

We had endured many odours on the way: rotting leaves, stagnant water, dung in all its odorous stages, animal urine. But this was different.

At first the men behind us laughed and teased each other, demanding to know who had relieved himself so stinkily right on the trail, but very quickly the smell became so pungent they had to stop their joking and cover their noses.

The Americans shouted something at Kinyo and my brother turned to Father.

'We have arrived.'

The steep slope led down to a flat clearing that narrowed to a cut between two mountains with only enough space for a single horseman to pass through. Where were the bodies? There was nothing in the pass but grey logs scattered everywhere and small black clouds of blowflies hovering over everything.

And then I realized. It was not wood that was strewn across the rock but dead men. The blowflies were feasting on the dead.

34

These corpses are just empty shells, I told myself. Their souls had fled long ago. Besides, I never knew these dead men. They were nothing to me.

And yet at the sight of those flyblown bodies, a terrible sorrow cut into me. It thrust deep into my belly then twisted up to spear my heart. I clapped a hand over my mouth to stifle the sounds suddenly bubbling up my throat. But it was no use. Tears were streaming from my eyes and when Kinyo asked, 'What's the matter, Samkad?' I could only shake my head, clamping my lips tightly together to stop the howl threatening to escape.

'Sam?' Father's voice was gentle. I felt his hand on my shoulder.

I pulled away, ashamed of my tears. I wanted to run away and hide, but now my knees were shaking and I had to crouch down on my haunches, both hands covering my mouth, my wet face hidden in my shoulder. These were not our dead! Why did my eyes want to weep for strangers? I rubbed my nose on my shoulder and wished that I had never come.

'Corporal Quinlan is asking what is the matter,' Kinyo whispered. 'What should I say, Father?'

Father didn't answer. He just knelt and put an arm around me. It was a comfort – even though the day was too hot to be so close to another human being – the grief in my throat stilled.

'I want to go home,' I mumbled.

Father held me closer. 'Not long now and we will be going home,' he said gently, 'When today is finished, we will return to the forest and the Americans will show us where they buried the Mangili. Then we can take Tambul's head back. Bury him complete. So that his soul will find peace in the world of the dead.'

The Americans' voices were rumbling all around us now. 'They're getting impatient!' Kinyo said urgently.

'Tell them . . .' Father paused to think. 'Tell them to go ahead, but Sam will remain here. We don't need him to help with the digging. And when the Americans no longer need your tongue, I want you to return and keep your brother company.'

Kinyo spoke Father's words . . . and the Americans laughed. The sound made me squirm with shame, and fresh grief stabbed so deep that I almost cried out. I heard Corporal Quinlan speak, his deep voice light with amusement.

'What is he saying?' Father said angrily. 'Why are they laughing?'

'He says,' Kinyo's voice broke, 'why are your children so squeamish when you people thrive on the stink of death? He says if we don't mind displaying a headless corpse then our children shouldn't mind a few more dead bodies.'

For a heartbeat, Father was silent. It filled me with an awful terror. What if Father leapt up to defend our honour only to be murdered by American guns? But he just leaned close and whispered in my ear. 'Stay here, son. Do not let this trouble you. It is right to mourn the dead.' He patted my back and stood up.

And so there I remained, crouching by the side of the trail, as the men processed down to the desolate pass where they would have to dig a grave deep enough to contain so many dead. I could not bear to return their curious glances so I threw my arms over my head.

When the sounds of passing feet had long passed, I attempted to stand. My knees were still soft and I stumbled a little as I crossed to the shadow of a boulder where I could wait for Kinyo to join me. I lowered myself carefully to the ground. Sorrow was a kind of pain, I realized. I could feel its wound, deep inside me, heavy and burning. Perhaps the death of Tambul had been the first cut. Perhaps losing my friend had made it easier for me to mourn total strangers.

It was a long, narrow incline to level ground. I could see vast wet patches of sweat blooming on the blue of the Americans' clothes. The heat made the odour of decay even more intense and they were holding squares of cloth over their noses. The Americans were shouting their commands even though nobody could understand them until Kinyo had translated their words.

Some of the men had already begun to dig, their bodies glinting with perspiration. The others were dragging corpses into piles, scattering the clouds of flies.

I'd never seen a place like this. The mountains huddled too close, sheer walls of stone plunging down to the rocky landing below. No gentle inclines here – everything was straight up and straight down, and anyone could see that it was a trap, that it was not a place that was easy to flee. You could only double back on the steep incline we'd arrived by or slip out through a narrow passage between two fingers of black stone where the horses were grazing on a stubble of brown grass. How did anyone come to decide this was a good place for a battle? It was only good for death.

I must have fallen asleep because when I opened my eyes Kinyo was standing in front of me.

My brother was staring down at me with a strange look on his face.

'Look away if you can only shame me with your stare,' I mumbled, closing my eyes to shut the sight of him away.

'Samkad, wake up.'

'I am awake.' I opened one eye. And then both eyes. There

was something wrong. Kinyo's eyes were red. His hands were trembling.

I sat up straight. 'Are you all right? Have the dead made you sad too?'

He shook his head.

I peered at him. He seemed paler. Like he had just been visited by a newly dead corpse.

He let out a deep sigh and clenched his fists.

'I hate them.'

'Who?'

'The Americans.'

'I thought they were your friends.'

'Mister William *is* my friend. But these Americans . . .' He shook his head. 'Down in the lowlands, in our village, they made us do this too, you know.'

'Do what?'

'Bury the dead. They marched us to a field where there had been a battle. Men, women, children, they didn't care how old we were. The bodies had been there for a few days and were bloated – arms and legs poking up, rigid. When I close my eyes, I can still see their dead stares. And do you know what was worse? Wherever the dead had lain, the grass had died too.' He shuddered. 'Afterwards, the field was covered with brown patches shaped like their bodies.'

'Did they give you guns?'

He looked away. 'We were lowlanders – the enemy. It was a punishment, not a job. Besides, they knew we'd been helping the soldiers of their enemy. Feeding them. Hiding them. That was why they burned our village.' He scowled. 'I hate them.'

'I stared at him. 'But you . . . you ate all those sweets!'

Kinyo almost smiled. 'Well, I do love sweets!'

'Why are you here? Don't they need you anymore?'

The almost-smile faded. 'They are asleep. Well . . . Private Henry and Private Smith are asleep. Corporal Quinlan is standing watch.' He pointed.

The two Americans were lying with their hats over their faces on the far end of the rocky space. A huge boulder cast a long, cool shadow over them. But the boulder blocked their view of the men at work. Corporal Quinlan sat on the other side of the boulder, keeping watch over the digging men. The horses were still cropping grass by the two fingers of rock. I could just see the tiny figure of Juan, crouched behind them, holding his hands over his head, to shade himself from the sun.

'Samkad.' There was something in the way my brother called my name that made the hairs rise on my arms. 'Sam, I have to tell you something.'

'What?'

Kinyo took a deep breath. 'Sometimes, the Americans forget I understand them.'

Private Henry had asked Corporal Quinlan sulkily if they really had to travel all the way back to the village. The American had laughed in response, as if the other man had made the funniest joke in the world.

'Corporal Quinlan called him an idiot,' Kinyo whispered.

'Once the job is done, we're going home, he said. Why should we go back to that village, he said. Private, have you forgotten, he said, that we *didn't* killed the Mangili?'

'I don't understand,' I gasped, panic rising in my throat. 'How can that be? If that is true then we left the village unprotected!'

Kinyo just looked at me with gaunt eyes.

The Americans had been lying to us all along.

35

I threw myself down the mountain. I had to tell Father. We had to go back. The village was in danger.

'Sam!' Kinyo cried. 'Wait!'

But there was no time to lose – what horrors had already happened while we were calmly meandering from mountain to mountain? *You are too late.* The thought slipped into my brain. *No!* I groaned. *Let it not be so!* But the words drummed in my head like the beat of a gangsa. *Too late. Too late. Too late.*

How the Mangili must have laughed from their hiding place when they saw us leaping to do the Americans' bidding.

The path levelled off a little bit and I raced on, half shutting my eyes to blur the sight of bodies lying in stacks, like logs. Overhead I noticed, for the first time, carrion birds, circling. The hum of the blowflies deepened as if they were pleased I had come and would I like to have a peek at a corpse or two?

Over by the boulder, Corporal Quinlan was watching me.

I slowed my feet, walked as if nothing urgent had propelled me down the mountain. As if I was just a boy wandering down to have a word with his father.

There were piles of gravel and dirt everywhere. The ditch was already knee high.

'Looking for your father, Samkad?' One of the men called. 'He's over there.'

Father was standing right in the middle of the grave, stabbing the ground with his stick. I jumped in and, keeping my voice low, told him the awful truth. The Americans had never met the Mangili. They had not killed anyone. There was no grave to dig up. No head in a basket to retrieve.

'Father,' I whispered. 'We should go back.'

But the eyes that met mine were round with horror. Father looked . . . terrified.

He exhaled. 'It's all right. They will let us go when we finish work.'

How could he say that? 'Father!' I insisted. 'We should go right away! What if—'

Father's digging stick clattered in the dirt. He stared at it. 'They – they will kill us, Sam,' he whispered. 'We can't get away.'

'There are twenty Bontok here and only three Americans!' Even as I said it I remembered Tambul's friend, Muddo, proposing exactly the same thing when the Americans had first arrived. And we should have, I thought, as Father shook his head. We should have defeated them then. 'Don't you care, Father? Don't you care that the Mangili will take the village?'

Father's chin sank into his chest. 'It's too late. Too late . . .'

'Samkad!' somebody above us hissed. 'Look at what your boy Kinyo is doing!'

Somehow Kinyo had obtained an axe and was dragging it towards the horses, the blade cutting a stripe in the dirt behind him. Corporal Quinlan was on his feet, shouting something in American.

But Kinyo ignored him, calling to Juan in the lowlander's tongue. When the prisoner held out his shackled wrists, Corporal Quinlan bolted into a run.

But there was a digging stick suddenly in the way and the American pitched forward into the dirt.

When Corporal Quinlan turned to yell at the owner of the digging stick, there was nobody there. The men watched innocently from a safe distance.

By now Kinyo had succeeded in severing the shackles that bound Juan's wrist's together and was trying to help the low-lander mount the nearest horse, which happened to be Corporal Quinlan's. Juan pulled himself up only to slip down the horse's other side. He grabbed the horse's mane with both hands, dragging himself back up to sprawl across its back like an ungainly monkey.

Kinyo, meanwhile, was slapping the beast's flanks and clicking his tongue. But the beast seemed unimpressed, taking a few dainty steps before coming to a stop and leaning down to nibble on a tuft of grass.

Corporal Quinlan drew his gun and aimed. There was a sharp report – but the bullet found no target. A stone had flown out of nowhere and struck the American's elbow, spoiling his aim.

And it was too late because Kinyo, waving and slapping the horse, had succeeded in herding the beast with the lowlander astride it through the two stone fingers to freedom.

Corporal Quinlan was roaring like an injured animal. He lifted his gun and pointed it at my brother.

But before he could fire, he crumpled, moaning to the ground. He tried to get back on his feet, muttering angrily under his breath.

And I swung Father's digging stick again.

And this time, when Corporal Quinlan fell to the ground, he stayed there.

Kinyo's face was livid. He ran towards me, screaming. It was a moment before I realized that the words roaring out of his throat were American. I looked over my shoulder to see Private Henry and Private Smith emerging from behind their boulder, their slowly-waking faces bewildered as they spotted Corporal Quinlan's still body on the ground.

Kinyo grabbed Private Henry's arm, shouting in a panicked voice. The American broke into a run towards the horses. Except there were no horses. Private Henry scratched the back of his head before he stumbled through the fingers of rock, chasing Juan on foot. Smith knelt next to Quinlan and rolled the unconscious man over. The men of Bontok turned to the grave and continued with their digging.

Kinyo leaned towards me. 'Samkad,' he whispered urgently. 'Let us go home. Now.'

Part Three
How to Be a Man

36

Father did not resist when Kinyo and I pulled him along; he ran obediently at our heels. I thought he was all right, but glancing over my shoulder, I realized that his eyes were glazed. He was as good as dream-walking.

'I told the Americans it was Juan who did it. The men helped me free the horses so that they couldn't chase the lowlander,' Kinyo panted. 'I told them it was the lowlander who knocked Corporal Quinlan down and then rode away.'

I was astonished into silence. When did the others decide that the Americans were their enemy? When did they decide that the lowlander was a friend?

We could hear a distant roaring behind us. Perhaps those great stone walls that plunged down into that dying place had collapsed in on themselves. Perhaps it was the clamour of angry men. I could look, I supposed. I could turn and climb up to that rock over there to see how that part of the story was ending.

But I didn't. I was afraid to know.

It seemed forever since the ancients had summoned me to declare me a man. How little I had known then. I had not known what a lowlander looked like. I had not known there was such a thing as America. I had not known it possible for there to be people with hair a colour other than black and skin a colour other than brown. I had not known that other throats fashioned entire languages that had no similarity to mine.

All these things I did know now, but I felt like one of those magic vessels that could never be full in those stories told by the ancients. I felt like I could never know enough.

Small avalanches of gravel bit into the soles of our feet. A gusting wind followed us up that long, rocky slope, prodding our backs with hard fingers, panting, *hurry, hurry, hurry. Away, away, away.*

'This is my fault,' Father muttered.

I touched his elbow. 'No, Father. We were betrayed.'

But Father shook his head. 'We allowed them to lie to us.' His words stabbed with the same rhythm as our footsteps. 'We did not resist, we did not question, we allowed it to happen. I was their fool.'

As we retraced our way home, Father would not be comforted. He continued to accuse himself.

I left him to it. Because he was right. We had allowed ourselves to be betrayed. How I had preened when Father told me I had become a man. I had believed him, believed that I was ready for it all. But what kind of man would make such an enormous mistake as to believe a lie?

With just the three of us the journey took half the time. Now the traverses between mountains seemed shorter, the gorges shallower. Even the river, as we crossed it, seemed still and meek, the water only gently licking at our feet.

Hurry, hurry, hurry. I was surprised to find that Kinyo was running comfortably alongside me. It was Father who lagged behind.

The sun was dying by the time we reached the mossy forest. It ignited everything with its last light. Under the forest canopy, shafts of sunlight hung like yellow fangs over our heads.

'We should stop to make some torches,' I called to Kinyo.

But even as I said it, I realized that there would be no need.

The trees were glowing.

The drip-drip of moss from the spreading branches over our heads oozed red. Light shuddered in the gaps of the trees. When we reached the forest's open mouth, where the village path began, it radiated with a strange leaping red light.

We walked out of the forest to see smoke rolling down the mountain.

We were too late. The village was on fire.

37

The fire snapped its fingers and flung sparks into the air. I could feel it burning in my eyes. It stained us red all over.

Too late, was all I could think, my mind dazed by the smoke and the heat. *Too late*. There was no village to save. No ancients. No people. Nobody.

Father fell to his knees. And then he was howling, his face pressed into the dirt, the sound spiralling from deep inside him. I turned away – I couldn't watch his pain.

Suddenly I saw something on the downward path – a quick shadow, blown along by the rolling heat. Then, something solid careered into my belly and suddenly I was gasping with joy. Black fur and pink tongue and desperate, desperate love. It was Chuka. Alive. Safe.

Kinyo grabbed me, turned me around. 'What do we do?' he cried. 'We've got to do something!'

I touched Father's back. 'Father?' I begged. 'Tell us what to do.' But only groaning noises moaned from his throat

I stared fearfully at the flames stabbing into the black of the sky. What if there were still people in the village?

'We must go in,' I said. 'People might be trapped and need our help. Kinyo, help me with Father.' We tried to pull Father to his feet, but he was immoveable, a stone clinging to the earth.

'My fault . . .' he moaned. 'All my fault.'

'Please,' I gasped. 'Please, Father.'

I grabbed his elbow and Kinyo took Father's other arm and together we raised him, forced him to put one foot in front of another. Chuka raced ahead. There was a strange pitch to her barking, like a warning. As if she was crying: 'Alert! Alert! Alert!'

Kinyo and I had to hold Father up, his body seemed to have no will of its own. Slowly, we made our way to the top, the air burning hotter and hotter as we climbed. Halfway there, we found Chuka waiting next to the bodies of two men, prone on the ground. Their heads had been taken.

'Don't look, Kinyo,' I commanded. 'Just don't look.' But Kinyo had already looked.

Father staggered to one of the bodies, rolled it over. He traced the tattoo of a snake on the man's chest. 'Dipa,' he whispered. 'It's Dipa.'

He touched the other man. 'This is Lamang. See, he has a small lizard on his shoulder.'

He bent over, covering his face with his hands, and this time, his sobs rose higher.

Father's weeping was tempting tears into my own eyes. But I blinked them away. *Don't allow yourself to feel, Sam. You must keep going.*

'Come on, Father,' I said firmly. Kinyo and I pulled Father to his feet and we continued to the top of the slope. Tambul was still there, now collapsed sideways in his death chair. But all the red of the fire had clouded over. Everything was bleached of colour. The grass and the path. The low stone wall. The trees. Everything was covered with a white dusting of ash.

Beyond the low wall, every single roof was ablaze. The fern tree pillars along the path smoked like torches, their buffalo skulls hung awry. Thick gouts of smoke puffed from more houses beyond.

My heart was pounding. Were there any people trapped in their houses?

Some of the bamboo poles making up Tambul's chair had sagged free. I let go of Father and unfastened the poles from the chair. 'Here.' I handed one to Kinyo. 'We must make sure nobody's caught in the fire.'

Kinyo and I moved quickly from house to house, using the poles to prod open scorched doors. We shouted into sheets of flame. 'Is there anybody there? Does anybody need help?'

There was no answer. Did that mean that they all got away? Were they safely in the caves? Or were they dead and quietly burning in their houses?

I whistled for Chuka. 'Dog, see if you can find anyone!' But she whined and shied away from the guttering huts.

The smoke was thickest near the House for Men. Flames rose out of the thatched roof in great sheets and under the burning rafters the skulls of our enemies glared at us.

'Sam, look!' Kinyo gasped.

There, in the middle of the courtyard, lay Mister William's music box.

Kinyo knelt and gathered it up in his arms, his face twisting with grief. 'They killed him too! They killed Mister William!'

There was a strange grumbling sound. The House for Men trembled. I grabbed Kinyo's arm and dragged him away just as the roof caved in, sending up a great cloud of sparks and smoke. Chuka howled as the flames swooped high into the black sky.

Father appeared in the smoke. 'We must get away from here!'

'But . . . the music box,' Kinyo cried.

'It is lost,' I said. 'Come on, Kinyo.'

We ran, coughing, Chuka chasing at our heels, until the path narrowed and we entered the First Valley.

The rice paddies flickered spookily in the firelight.

Father slowly sat on his heels, his face gaunt.

'We didn't find anybody in the houses,' I said softly. 'Perhaps everyone managed to flee.'

Father whispered, 'The spirits of our ancestors are gone. Chased away by the fire. We have no one to protect us now.'

He tore at his hair as his eyes searched the sky. 'Mother! Uda! Are you still with us?' He covered his eyes. 'She's not here. I can feel it. She has left us. They all have.'

I threw my arms around Father, trying to lift him up again. 'Father, let us go to the cave. Everyone will be there.'

'There is no use. I am no good to anyone any more,' he whispered. 'I have lost my courage.'

Kinyo grabbed his hand, but he pushed my brother away. 'There are only enemy spirits here now. I can feel them. They are walking alongside us.'

Chuka nuzzled Father's knee, and Father gathered the dog close to him, burying his face in her neck for a long moment.

Father looked at me, smiling sadly. 'She's a good dog,' he said. 'A fierce dog.'

He ran his hands down Chuka's flanks and she arched with pleasure.

'You love my son, don't you, dog?' Father said.

Chuka smiled as if she understood.

'You would do anything for him, wouldn't you? You would chase away the evil spirits that plague us, if you could.' Father's voice was sing song, as if he was chanting a prayer.

He turned Chuka round to face us, his arm circling the dog's body.

'Will you do this for us?' he whispered into her ear. 'Will you help us? We need allies in the world of the spirits. My dog, Asin, will meet you and he will help you fight the spirits of our enemies.'

He wrapped a hand around Chuka's snout and, clamping her mouth shut, pinned her wriggling body with his elbow and drew his axe.

38

We send the souls of beasts to the spirits all the time. To learn the portents, to thank our ancestors for a good harvest, to look after the souls of the newly dead, to chase away the wicked spirits – Chuka's fierce soul would have called our ancestors back and defended us from the enemy spirits that had overwhelmed the village.

And yet, I couldn't let Father kill her.

I found myself lunging across the void, throwing myself between the warm, wriggling body of my dog and Father's axe.

'Sam!' Father looked strange with tears carving wet trails down his brown cheeks. The axe wavered above our heads. 'I beg you, let me do this. It's the only way. We are helpless here in the land of the living. We must fight the Mangili from the land of the dead. The dog is our only hope.'

'No!' I had my arms around Chuka now. I tried to free her

from Father's grip – or at least put myself between her and his axe. 'Go, dog. Run.'

Chuka wriggled, trying to flee, but Father's fist was tight around her leg. He pushed me to the ground with his elbow and pulled her close. 'I'm sorry, son.'

But the axe was snatched from Father's hand.

Kinyo ran down the embankment and swung his arm in a wide arc. The axe sailed into the shadows below us. There was a distant splash.

'Foolish boy,' Father cried, fists clenched. Chuka threw herself away from him and scurried down the embankment, disappearing off into the lower terraces.

'Run, Kinyo, to the cave!' I cried, finding my feet. 'Father, please, come with us!'

But Father didn't seem to hear – he stood, staring blindly across the valley. He looked like he was dream walking again.

We could not wait for Father to wake himself. I hurried after Kinyo. The narrow twisting paths on top of the embankment were slippery under our running feet. 'Hurry,' I gasped. 'Hurry.' The light fell away rapidly as we left the village behind us.

Soon it became so dark we had to slow down. I had walked the terraces often enough to remember the turns of the embankment path, but Kinyo had never done it before. I took his hand and we crept along, feeling our way.

'The ridge between the valleys is up these steps,' I called.

'What steps? It's too dark.'

'This way, when we get to the top, we'll be in the next rice valley where the cave is.'

But we had not yet reached the top when a hand clamped over my mouth.

A fist closed painfully on my wrist.

'Don't go into the valley, Samkad, it's too dangerous,' Little Luki breathed into my ear. 'You'll be totally useless without your head.'

39

The paddy water lay still over my shoulders like a funeral shawl.
I could see smoke seething in the sky above us, lit red by fire,
but the paddy water was bone cold and I heard Kinyo gasp as
Luki urged him lower into the water. 'Hush,' Luki whispered.
'They will hear you.'

I could feel coarse, stalky things under my toes and my
elbow sank deep in mud. Something wriggled over my arm. I
closed my eyes, trying not to think of snakes.

'Down, down,' Luki said quietly. 'Get as low as you can.'

We planted ourselves deep in the paddy. I tilted my head
back so that it was just my nostrils and my mouth showing
above the black water.

Where had Luki been all this time? How had she come
to be here? I looked across at my friend. There was nothing to
see, of course, just black things against black in the black water.

When we were small, running naked in the dirt alleys of the village, it was always Luki I had wanted to play with. Always Luki I had preferred over the other children as we copied the grown-ups, banging on gangsas made of sticks and stones, hunting the chickens and dogs as if they were wild boar, taking the heads of our make-believe enemies with our make-believe axes. There was no reason to change the way we played when our elders declared it time for me to wear a breechcloth and Luki to wear a skirt. It had not occurred to me that our paths would have to change, even when it came time for the Cut and I was about to become someone else forever. I had not known how to be a friend to Luki the way she had been a friend to me. The realization brought such an ache to my breast that I gasped.

'Shut up,' Luki whispered. 'They're coming.'

I leaned my cheek on some bracken and allowed a slice of ear above the water to listen. I could hear someone groaning. And the soft thud of feet on the packed dirt on top of the paddy wall.

I rolled over onto my belly and eased my head carefully over the embankment to look. The glow from the burning village lit three men above us on the ridge.

One was Mister William. Even by the wavering light I could see that his face was bruised – one eye was swollen shut.

I stared hungrily at the two Mangili who were with him. All my life I had imagined what our blood enemy would look like. Father told me the Mangili had bright red lips, they spoke in an alien tongue and they washed the bones of their dead. But these were ordinary men, golden-skinned, muscled and black-haired. Dressed in breechcloths like any man from Bontok, with tattoos across their chests.

There was a rough shout – one of the Mangili pulled Mister William down to his knees. The other grabbed him by the hair and yanked his head back with a savage jerk. They were going to take Mister William's head.

But then one of the shadows gathering beside them lunged, head-butting the Mangili who was about to relieve the American of his head. The Mangili toppled into the water.

My heart was pounding. It was Father who had struck the Mangili . . . but it was a clumsy attack because Father fell into the water too and, what with the mud and the flailing axe of the Mangili in the water next to him, Father could not get back on his feet, slipping and sliding and falling over in the paddy.

By the time the other Mangili thought to swing his axe at Mister William and finish what they had set out to do, the American had rolled out of reach and into the two other men's watery struggle.

'Stones!' I yelled to Luki and Kinyo, clambering out of our hiding place to grope for missiles on the path. I lobbed a stone at the Mangili still hovering on the embankment, but I got my aim wrong and it struck Mister William, who dropped into the water.

The Mangili pushed Father against the paddy wall. He was

too close to swing the axe so he pushed his body against Father, using elbow and shoulder to batter him. As he moved back to make room to swing his axe, the other man hurried over to help. Out of the water shot Father's arm, grabbing the end of the Mangili's breechcloth. With one yank, he was lying across Father like a shield, taking his friend's axe blade deep between his shoulders.

I was trying to get closer, throwing stones as I crossed the mud wall to the paddy where the battle was taking place. But in the dark my stones flew in wrong directions, pelting wide and low. Mister William was staggering back onto his feet when one struck him on the forehead. I groaned as the American fell like a tree.

'Stop! Stop!' I heard Luki cry, close behind me.

Father had seen us. 'Get out!' he roared. 'Get away from here!'

And allow you to be killed, Father? It would be wrong. If only I had an axe.

I blinked. Was that an axe on the paddy wall? For a heart-beat, I wondered if some helpful spirit had granted my wish. Then I remembered. The dead Mangili had dropped it when Father pulled him into the water.

I grabbed it and jumped into the paddy, vaguely hearing Luki scream, 'No, Samkad, don't!'

A thud. A gasp. I was too late. I stared down to find Father looking up at me. His face a spatter of blood. His eyes fixed on mine. Pleading, loving, afraid. His lips moved. What was he

227

saying? What was he trying to tell me? His eyes began to glaze, the lids fluttering down, closing. The waters rolled over his face as he sank into the paddy water.

The Mangili was fishing Father out of the water, straddling him. He pushed Father's chin up, baring his neck. He glanced sideways at me. He must have been about Tambul's age, with a similar sinewy build. He was handsome, with a straight nose, full lips and thick dark brows over dark brown eyes. He was a young man like any other.

He laughed at the sight of me. Perhaps he thought it funny, a small boy like me coming to the rescue. Perhaps it was the way I struggled to lift the axe.

It was heavy. But I could lift it.

I closed my eyes and swung the axe as hard as I could.

40

The ancients are always saying they can't wait to die. When they die, they say their souls are going to join the world of the spirits. No more aches and pains, no more wrinkles, no more mashing your rice because your teeth have fallen out. And once they had become part of the invisible world, they could watch over the rice valleys, whispering to the green shoots to grow fat and tall. In the invisible world, they could protect their families from illness and danger. In the invisible world, they could live forever.

When Corporal Quinlan forced Luki back into the mossy forest, it was the spirits who led her to climb a tree, to hide her shame, to weep her disappointment. It was the spirits who made sure she saw the two Mangili creeping through the forest so that she could hurry back to the village to tell the ancients.

When Kinyo, Father and I fled, leaving the men behind

with the Americans, it was the spirits who gave them courage to ignore the gun that Private Smith's trembling hands pointed at them. It was the spirits who told them to lay down their tools, leave the Americans, and make their way home.

There were wicked spirits about as well, whispering into Dipa and Lamang's ears so that they laughed and turned their backs on Luki. It was the wicked spirits who told them their new guns could protect them from any Mangili.

But where were the spirits now? Was Father right? Had the fire driven all the spirits away? Were we now orphaned and powerless against our enemies?

It was difficult not to think so.

It was hard, trudging into the smoking ruins of the village, every building a mangled, smouldering black thing, shelter and hope and safety long evaporated into the stinking air. This was what enemies did. They destroyed homes. The Americans had destroyed the homes of the lowlanders. And now the Mangili had done the same to us.

The village was already on fire when Little Luki realized that Mister William was missing. And so there was no spirit to guide her when she stole out of the cave. No spirit led her through the burning houses where she found the American cowering behind one of the buildings. No spirit to warn her that the Mangili were following as she led Mister William across the First Valley. And when she realized this, there was no spirit to help when Mister William panicked and was easily caught by the enemy, while Luki quickly melted into the waters of a rice paddy.

We roamed the village in silence, staring hopelessly at the wreckage. Agkus stood silently with her arms around Kinyo. They had fled to the mountains to escape the horrors in the lowlands only to find more death and devastation.

'It is not houses that make a village, but the hearts that beat within it,' Salluyud declared, as he shuffled slowly with us.

But when the ancients saw the pile of ashes that used to be the House for Men, they could think of no more wise words. Suddenly they had no comfort to give us, no ritual to make.

How could they offer up pleas to the spirits if there was nobody there to listen?

'Look, Sam,' Little Luki said. 'What is Chuka doing?'

Chuka's head was poking out from under the charred beams of a ruined hut. I waited for her to bound up to me, plant her paws on my chest. But she leaped out of the hut, barked, then jumped back in again, looking over her shoulder to check if I was following.

'What is it?' I followed slowly.

She grabbed a fallen piece of wood and pulled it aside.

Deep in its stone pen, safe and unburned, was a pig. It stared up at me with its little eyes and coughed.

One pig. Alive.

The entire village descended to the mossy forest. Luki

walked with her mother, Chochon, and Kinyo with his aunt, Agkus. Mister William trudged behind them, his head bound where my stones had accidentally struck.

Kinyo was right – *this* American was not the enemy. That strange, burning night, I had dragged Father out of the paddy. My hands had pressed at the gash in his shoulder, trying to stop his soul from soaking into the shadows of the paddy wall. *Too late again, Samkad*, I had told myself. Father was dying and soon would become one of the Uninvited.

But then Mister William was there, tearing strips from his own clothes to bind Father's shoulder. He stopped the bleeding and Father did not die and Mister William was constantly at Father's side now, at the rough encampment that would have to be home until we rebuilt our houses.

I looked around me like I was seeing the woods for the first time. Every leaf, every dripping strand of moss, every branch seemed aglow with the new sun's light.

Everything was alive.

The Tree of Bones called loudly. *One pig, alive*, the voices hummed. *And men, women and children. All alive.*

We stood under the tree, and joined the ancients in calling up to the spirit figures that gazed benevolently upon us with their white pebble eyes.

It is not houses that make a village, but the hearts that beat within it. This was the thing to celebrate.

41

Father lived to see the village celebrate the three of us children as heroes. He lived to see Kinyo and me safely ensconced in the new House for Men, our foreskins cut.

He lived to see Salluyud take his buffalo horn with the three lemon thorns on it and tap a fine tattoo of a caterpillar across my chest, to show that I had defeated my enemy. He lived to see the ancients grant Luki special tattoos on both shoulders that acknowledged her as a fighter. They did offer Kinyo a tattoo as well, for his courage, but he didn't want one.

He lived to see the village rebuilt. He lived to see Mister William's house, with its wide porch and a blackboard on the wall. He lived to attend three lessons on how to speak Mister William's tongue. But he said he was too old and too ill to learn the new words.

He lived . . . and then he died, because even Mister William's potions could not heal his festering wounds. Perhaps Mother had become tired of waiting and beckoned his spirit away to join her in the invisible world. Father had a good death. A natural death.

We mourned Father correctly. We sat him in his death chair. We covered his shoulders with a funeral shawl. We spoke to his corpse. We addressed the spirits politely and sang the correct songs. And then we buried him next to the house we built after the fire, the house where someday I will live with my wife, when I decide to marry.

The Tree of Bones calls.

See, see, it whispers. *See how Bontok glows in the morning sun, the green of the terraces, the swirling blue of the Chico River, the jungles that nestle in every crook and elbow of the mountains. See the tiny village, that once sat unnoticed on the mountain's knee. Now discovered. See the new road, a white ribbon cutting its way through the old forest. See the new houses springing up along the road. See the new people, moving in from everywhere.*

See the soldiers, the Tree of Bones whispers. *Our warriors now march about in smart American hats and smart American shirts and smart American belts with American guns on their shoulders. The only thing that reminds us of who they once were are the breechcloths that swing between their bare legs.*

See Mister William's house, where the villagers sit and listen to him talk about America, a land that is bigger than the whole of Bontok, than the mountains, than the lowlands. Where people live in clean boxes made of neat blocks of stone. Where they wear clothing on their backs and shoes on their feet.

Father told me Lumawig once took a clay pot and smashed it on the ground. It splintered into many shards. One of the shards was Bontok.

But Mister William has a map. And on his map, America is a giant cabbage-coloured shape in the middle. And Bontok is . . . not even on the map.

We thought the ancients could teach us everything we needed to know about our world. How to carve a rice field into a mountain. How to hunt deer and trap boar. How to fight our blood enemy, the Mangili.

But now the ancients nod and say the Mangili are no longer our enemy and we must all learn the ways of the American.

This pleases Mister William and he carefully unpacks his box and plays music for us. The ancients close their eyes and listen.

Look, whispers the Tree of Bones. *Mister William is showing the ancients how to measure time. A day is made of hours. A month is made of days. A year is made of months. And a man is made of years.*

Look, look, the Tree of Bones whispers. *See your brother, Kinyo. Kinyo wears white trousers and a white shirt. On his head is a straw hat. He works for an American and his wife who live in the lower village, near the river. They go from village to village exchanging squares of fabric they bought in the lowlands for everyday things. Pots. Bowls. Wooden stools. Spears. Shields. Earrings. Baskets. One day the wife tries to exchange a square of blue cloth for Chochon's snake-bone headband. The one Luki made for her. Chochon walks away.*

Look how Kinyo works. He counts their plates and spoons and forks. He boils their water to get rid of the evil spirits that might make them ill. He scrubs their wooden floor with half a coconut husk until it gleams.

See how these Americans love Kinyo, the Tree of Bones calls. *Do you hear what they're saying? They want to take him back to America with them. In fact, they say they want to take all of Bontok to America. To show Americans our way of living.*

See, the Tree of Bones calls. *Can you see?*

Epilogue

I cut the chicken's neck quickly. It struggles a little, but it tires soon enough as its blood soaks into the roots of the tree. I watch as its spirit leaves its body. Then I take it up the tree, picking my way carefully on the great sagging branches, slippery with moss.

The Tree of Bones sighs.

As I climb, Chuka whimpers down below, wishing me to hurry up with my task. Soon I am at the top. I push through the dense ceiling of leaves and tie the chicken firmly to a branch.

To one side, I can see the mountain flowing down to the caves. On the other side, there is a swirling fog in the valley. The tips of trees poke out like reeds in a river. I can see the rice paddies up and down the mountainside, tiers of them, flooded and ready for planting, glinting like the scales of a snake just after it sheds its old skin.

On the branch adjacent to me are two figures made of blackened tree fern. They sit side by side, their white pebble eyes gazing peacefully into the distance.

I say the words the ancients have taught me to honour the souls of my parents, my voice calm and strong. But the beat of my heart is quick and my chest aches. A day is made of hours. A month is made of days. A year is made of months. And a man is made of years. Five years have passed since Father died. And still, whenever I visit the Tree of Bones, I feel like a little boy again, lonely for my mother and father.

I whisper goodbye to the spirit figures. The wind gently shakes the tree and it tinkles its farewell as I make my way down.

'Samkad!'

Luki is waiting, just outside the tree's barrier. She is sitting on her heels, her arms wrapped around Chuka's neck. She is wearing a skirt and her hair is tied back with a string of beads. She is also wearing a white shirt, a gift from an American missionary. It looks bulky and strange, but Luki seems not to mind.

'Did you hear, Samkad? Kinyo's new American is asking who amongst us would like to go with him and his wife to America.'

'I heard.'

'So . . . are you going? Kinyo said he might.'

'Kinyo wishes *he* was American. Do you want to go?'

Luki shrugs. 'Maybe. I'd like to see America. Who knows if

what Mister William says is true. He could tell us anything and we would never know if he was making it up.'

I make a face. 'America sounds . . . different. What if they make us wear shoes? Or if they take away our axes? What if they make us speak only their language?'

'Haven't you noticed? They're doing that already!' she laughs. 'Anyway, I'm not here to talk about Americans. I wanted to show you something.'

She holds it up. I frown. Its a plaited vine fastened to a wooden handle.

'What is it?'

'It's a sling! I made it yesterday. Watch!'

Chuka complains as Luki pushes her aside to get to her feet. She loads a stone into the end of the sling and peers at the trees around us. 'There! See that papaya?'

The papaya tree has a long, gangly trunk with a head of unruly leaves. It is growing at an angle, bending away from the shadows and reaching for the sun like a pointing finger amid the lush masses of fern trees and shrubs. A single papaya nestles at its neck.

'Watch!' Grasping the handle, Luki whirls the sling above her head.

Snap! The papaya drops to the ground.

I grin at Luki. 'Great shot!'

'The handle gives it more accuracy and power!' Luki smiles.

The early morning sun edges higher, and everything seems to burst into flame instantaneously. Little Luki's long black hair is crowned with gold. The back of her long neck is molten with sunlight. Her white blouse is askew and I can see the beginnings of one bare shoulder.

'Why are you looking at me like that?' Luki snaps.

'Nothing.' But I can't look away.

Suddenly Luki swings her leg in a circle, sweeping my feet from under me. I fall to the ground and before I can grab her, Luki's got my arm twisted behind my back. Chuka yelps, but she doesn't move to intervene. And then we are grappling. We are rolling in the dirt until we smack against the fencing around the Tree of Bones. Luki is surprisingly strong considering that I'm head and shoulders taller than her now. I hear Luki's plaintive voice from a long time ago. *You're too short to carry a shield. You're smaller even than a wild boar – how are you supposed to spear one? And look at your arms! They're like twigs. How are you going to chop off the heads of the Mangili?* I begin to laugh, even though Luki's arm is now wrapped around my throat. My arms no longer look like twigs. And Luki is no longer Little Luki with that mango face.

Luki rolls me onto my back, expertly pinning my arms down with her knees, her forearm across my neck. But still I laugh, choking a little because it's hard to laugh with an arm across your throat.

Luki grins.

'I saw a boar near the caves yesterday when I was collecting firewood,' she says. 'It was huge! Shall we take Chuka and . . .' She raises an arm as if she is throwing a spear.

I laugh even harder. 'Chochon will be furious.'

'Huh!' Luki wrinkles her nose. 'She'd probably rather that I weave a blanket or boil a baby or something.'

'And the ancients will demand that you wear the itchiest, most womanly skirt available.'

She sticks her tongue out at me.

I smile. 'So . . . shall we meet here after breakfast?'

She gives me a quick slap on the cheek. 'I'll be there!'

And suddenly she's gone and there's Chuka, her paws on my chest, frantically licking my face, because my talking to Luki had made her lonely again.

The Tree of Bones chortles and somewhere I can hear the loud squawk of a hornbill.

A Note from the Author

Dear Reader,

This story is not history though it is set during a real time, in a real place. There really were headhunters in Bontok, and the United States really did invade the Philippines in 1899, just as its native people were beginning to call themselves Filipinos.

I read a lot of books from the period – which is known in the Philippines as the Philippine-American War, and in the United States as the Philippine Insurrection. But most of the information I could find was written by Americans, writing as tourists, anthropologists, conquerors. I could find no unfiltered Filipino voices telling our side of the story.

Gina Apostol, the Filipino author of *Gun Dealer's Daughter*, reports having the same experience while researching her novels. When she sought the Filipino voice, she said, she could only find it in 'a text within a text, mediated, annotated and translated by her enemy'. Writing this book made me realize that there is a world of stories in my native land that beg telling, and a multitude of voices that need to be heard.

Bone Talk is set in the magnificent highlands of the Philippines – a region called the Cordillera, populated by impressive folk who carved rice fields out of vertiginous mountains and, for three hundred years, repulsed invasions by both lowlanders and Spanish colonizers.

I do not hail from the Cordillera and I beg the forgiveness of its many and diverse peoples for any misreadings of their culture. As a storyteller I can only spin a pale imitation of any reality. I hope that this story awakens the world's curiosity about this extraordinary time and place.

With utmost respect to the people of the Cordillera,

Candy Gourlay

Acknowledgements

With thanks to the British Library, truly a Cave of Wonders, where I wrote most of this book.

Respect and gratitude to the people of the Cordillera, in particular Suzette Bencio and Jerome Che-es, who hosted me during my stays in Maligcong, answered all my questions and showed me what mountain hospitality is all about. Thanks, too, to Jeremy Pursen, who sat with us around a fire and told stories about the old ways. Thank you to his son, Perky Pursen, who guided us up a mountain in total darkness to watch the sun rise and a sea of clouds bubble up into the horizon. And thank you to the stalwart mountain dog, Kunig, who accompanied us on long walks and herded us along on the steep paths through the rice terraces.

With sincere thanks to the travel bloggers, Oggie Ramos and Ferdz Decena, through whose blogs I learned about the secret glories of Maligcong. Imagine my surprise to meet them in person, totally by chance staying at the same homestay!

I owe a debt to the long-ago men and women who wrote about their travels in turn-of-the-twentieth-century Philippines. I drew much detailed information from *The Bontoc Igorot* (1903) by Albert Jenks, who closely observed the people of Bontoc at the dawning of the American occupation of the Philippines – though it was from the diary and letters of his wife, Maude Huntley Jenks, that I found a more human and engaging picture of the Bontoc people. Her posthumous 1951 book, sensationally titled *Death Stalks the Philippine Wilds*, begins with disgust for the 'savages' she met in 1903, but ends with a warm affection for a people she had learned to love.

Respect and gratitude to the historian, William Henry Scott, who lived amongst the people of the Cordillera and made it his life's work to amplify the voices of our native peoples from the historical accounts that reduced them to voiceless sideshows.

Thank you to my friend, Gregg Jones, for meticulously chronicling the forgotten war between the Philippines and the United States in his book, *Honor in the Dust: Theodore Roosevelt, War in the Philippines, and the Rise and Fall of America's Imperial Dream.*

I am also grateful to Bel Castro for her essay 'Food Morality and Politics'; to my cousin, Susan Quimpo, who tried to help me get to grips with Philippine animism by lending me *The Soul Book* by Gilda Cordero Fernando, Francisco R. Demetrio and Fernando Zialcita, illustrated by Roberto B. Feleo; to the bloggers of *The Aswang Project*, especially Jordan Clark, whose constant interrogation of pre-Christian faiths and mythology helped me work out the belief systems of my characters. Thank you Xi Zuq for helping me seek out readers. Thank you Gawani for your feedback. Thank you, Cristina Juan of the School of Oriental and Asian Studies for her advice and support (especially for introducing me to the Bontok Talking Dictionary of the National Museum of Ethnology in Osaka, Japan), and to Bontoc film-maker, Mark Lester Menor Valle, who helped me find a name for my village's fictional enemy, the Mangili. Thank you also to Nash Tysmans, for her kind feedback as well as her vivid photography of one of the last remaining mossy forests in the Cordillera region.

Thank you to my trusted author friends who read and re-read my draft chapters: Cliff McNish, Joe Friedman, Helen Peters and Christina Vinall – their responses helped me find the words to bridge many cultural gaps. Last minute thanks to Mio Debnam for boar odour advice and friendship.

Thank you, Hilary Delamere, my ever-patient agent.

And thanks to the team at David Fickling Books for keeping faith with my impossible story.

Thank you, too, to my sister, Mia Quimpo, who walked the terraces with me.

And as always to my husband, Richard – whose thoughts about the measure of a man helped me find a way out of my story labyrinth.

THIS BOOK IS ENDORSED BY

Amnesty International endorses *Bone Talk* because it upholds many human rights, including our rights to life, to equality, to have a religion and enjoy our own culture. It also shows us what can happen when these are taken away from us.

Amnesty International is a movement of ordinary people from across the world standing up for humanity and human rights. Our purpose is to protect individuals wherever justice, fairness, freedom and truth are denied.

Bone Talk is set in 1899, but since 1948 we all have human rights, no matter who we are or where we live. The Universal Declaration of Human Rights (UDHR) was created after the horrors of World War II. It was the first document to agree common, global terms for truth, justice and equality. Human rights help us to live lives that are fair and truthful, free from abuse, fear and want and respectful of other people's rights. But they are often abused and we need to stand up for them, for ourselves and for other people. We can all help to make the world a better place, every day.

If you want to stand up for human rights, you can:

Find out how to start a Youth Group in your school or community at: www.amnesty.org.uk/youth

Join the Junior Urgent Action network at: www.amnesty.org.uk/jua

Take action online for individuals at risk around the world at: www.amnesty.org.uk/actions

If you are a teacher or librarian, you are welcome to use our many free resources for schools at: www.amnesty.org.uk/education

Amnesty International UK,

The Human Rights Action Centre,

17-25 New Inn Yard,

London

EC2A 3EA

Tel: 020 7033 1500

Email: sct@amnesty.org.uk

About the Author

Growing up in the Philippines, Candy Gourlay wondered why all the books she'd ever loved didn't resemble her steamy, tropical home in Manila. As a result, it took her years to fulfil her dream of becoming an author – and years to learn that Filipino stories, too, belong in the pages of books.

Candy's novels for young readers, *Tall Story* and *Shine*, have been listed for many prizes such as the Carnegie Medal and the Guardian Children's Book Prize. She lives in London with her family.